STRANGE ROOMS

*Speculative Works of the
Absurd and Macabre!*

Michal Leigh

Cover design by Michal Pfettscher
Interior design by Michal Pfettscher
Illustrations by Michal Pfettscher
First edition 2025

Published in the United States by Michal Leigh Pfettscher DBA Oddity Press
Copyright © 2025 Michal Pfettscher writing as Michal Leigh.

Library of Congress Control Number Pending

Paperback ISBN: 979-8-9990988-0-1
EPUB ISBN: 979-8-9990988-1-8

Contents:

Michal Leigh

Author's Note
*Content warning, disclaimer, acknowledgements,
and profuse apologies, all in one big, happy blob of
warm and friendly text:*

Readers, particularly the author's mother, should be
aware from the cover that this book does not contain
heartwarming tales from the life of a countryside veterinarian.
Nor does it contain uplifting spiritual allegories or the life-
affirming yarns of an experienced and wise traveler. In case the
cover didn't clue you in, these stories bear no resemblance to
James Harriot's, although I do know a person or two named
James. Some of the stories herein contain references to gore,
death and dismemberment, and other potentially triggering
themes.

Nothing contained within this book is intended to
condone violence in real life. And the content is not intended to
represent people or events from the author's real life. In fact,
she promises that she loves her husband very much and
absolutely does not have any plans to murder or dismember
him at the time of this writing. In other words, you can go to

1

sleep, Jonathon. I promise you're safe. Really. If I meant to do anything to you, it would have happened long ago.

I truly appreciate all the nights you read my stories only to shake your head and lovingly declare that I'm weird. You deserve a really giant soft pretzel and an absurdly long nap with a soft, morbidly obese cat whose wit and energy *almost* rival that of a threadbare shoelace.

To reiterate, the text within these pages is fictional writing meant for entertainment value. All characters and events represented in these works, including Elsie Munroe, are purely fiction and for entertainment purposes.

So, Mom, my mental health and relationships are fine. I'm not suffering emotionally from anything, and please don't put me on the prayer chain after reading this. In fact, I'm okay if you want to just stop here and let Dad read this one since I know it's not really your genre.

On the subject of genre, a few of the stories in this collection fit squarely within the horror category, most are speculative in nature, at least one is science fiction, a few are poignant, and several are simply absurd. The thing that ties them together is that they all center around a particular living space, in other words, a room.

We all have spaces in our mind that are private spaces, rooms that we do not share. Some are merely personal things that are in themselves fairly innocuous. One does not often discuss the state of one's hemorrhoids with friends and family for instance, but no one would think less of you for having them or thinking about them.

Other rooms, if unlocked, could permanently alter lives merely by allowing a crack of light to shine in. And if the doors were to be thrown open completely, well, that would simply be madness of the very worst kind. Intrusive thoughts, conspiracy theories, irrational fears, violent and sexual impulses, and the "call of the void" exist in the backrooms of every mind at some time or another. These are the rooms people keep shut because there are monsters lurking in them. Since the monsters are more often than not, our selves, most people prefer not only to lock the doors, but to pretend they don't even exist.

However a lack of suitability for daily use doesn't mean that these rooms aren't useful. They are stories within us. Stories allow us to live a thousand lives, both the stories we read and the stories we create in the secret places of our minds. Stories let us play the victim or the villain, the child with unlimited possibility or the ancient sage with secret wisdom. In stories, we can do or say or be anything at all. In choosing our stories, in a way, we choose our own reality.

These stories are keyholes in doors leading down a single, dark and narrow hall to which I have allowed you, my dear reader, access. Expert homemaker Elsie Munroe will be your escort via her housekeeping column.

"Who Is Elsie Munroe?" you might ask. Elsie Munroe,

then Elsie Green, and I met many years ago when she was a bright eyed premed student and I was to be her roommate.

Elsie was petite, blonde, and gave the impression of a wholesome, "Leave It To Beaver" type. Her sense of humor was odd but infectious. I particularly remember her mentioning, not five minutes after we'd introduced ourselves, that she had an interest in skin afflictions and abnormalities, and would genuinely like to see whenever I had any scabs.

At the time, I took this to be an eccentric sort of joke, but in time my assumption was proved wrong by the multiple declarations of, "You have to see this," preceding her shoving medical textbooks under my nose. The books usually featured full color photographs of blackened pustules or growths resembling cauliflower in varying states of decay.

Despite our different reading preferences, Elsie and I hit it off from the beginning. She was bubbly and warm in ways that most people only affect, but Elsie never gave off a bit of insincerity. In fact, I can't imagine anyone not liking Elsie immediately upon meeting her.

Elsie was a good roommate, kept her belongings tidy and clean, kept reasonable hours, and had no bad habits that I knew of. She always kept a variety of medicines on hand, which was useful whenever one of us got sick.

Elsie was a great encourager, and helped me through a breakup by lending me a lighter to burn everything of my ex-boyfriend's that remained after I broke up with him.

Interestingly enough, he died in an apartment fire the following week. Police said that he'd been drunk and fallen asleep with a cigarette. I found this odd, since I had never known him to drink or smoke, but Elsie told me that he must have picked up bad habits to cope with the guilt over his regretful treatment of me.

When I became her roommate, Elsie was a couple years ahead of me in school and was already seeing Tim, who would later become her first husband. They both graduated and were married the following year, though unfortunately it wasn't meant to be. Tim's rather wealthy family had just bought him a new Mercedes as a graduation present, and barely into the honeymoon, the brakes inexplicably failed. Elsie had been in their hotel suite at the time, and survived him as widow at barely 23 years of age.

Between some documents that Elsie and Tim had in place before the wedding and a legal settlement with Mercedes Benz, Elsie became independently wealthy to the degree that she could afford a modest lifestyle without having to maintain regular employment. Since then, Elsie has predominantly kept busy by simply being Elsie. She bakes, keeps house, gardens, crafts, and even keeps a science lab of some sort which she is evasive about. She was remarried, to Stuart Sims who died of a tragic hiking accident, and later Jeremiah Munroe whose death was deemed a case of accidental poisoning.

It was around the time of Mr. Munroe's funeral that I first learned of Elsie's writing talents. I came over with a platter of cold cuts to find Elsie sitting at an old-fashioned manual typewriter next to a stack of documents roughly eighteen inches in height. When I inquired as to what all the writing was for, Elsie merely stated that it was for her devoted readership who relied heavily on her advice in all matters in life.

While I'm entirely in the dark as to what publication her advice has appeared in, Elsie assures me that her readership is very loyal, and I did not think it wise to inquire further. I now leave you in her capable hands as your docent and chaperone in this gallery of strange rooms.

Enjoy the tour,

Michal Leigh

Michal Leigh

-1-

"NO PLACE LIKE HOME"

Home is Where the Heart Is

Elsie Munroe

"Home is where the heart is," the old adage goes. Our hearts are indeed at home, but why stop there? Home is the location of a myriad of body parts, including, but not limited to; spleens, livers, kidneys, intestines, and many more. There are several reasons one might consider not leaving these lying about though.

For one, they do tend to make guests uncomfortable. Of course, everybody has limbs and internal organs, and they are nothing to be ashamed of, but storing them in the open is something of a taboo in polite society. If you enjoy entertaining guests with any frequency, you will certainly need to take this into consideration.

Secondly, body parts can contribute to a cluttered appearance in the home. Seldom do tchotchke and knick-knack covered shelves grace the covers of home magazines. Modern design is sleek and often minimalistic, featuring simple or even monochromatic color schemes. Overall design should be prioritized over the aesthetic of individual pieces. Less is often more from a design standpoint.

Thirdly, the reduction of organs in the home reduces workload. Organs left in a common area have to be changed frequently, much like flowers in a vase. Without vigilant effort, even the most diligent of homemakers can find herself the victim of unpleasant odors. The seepage of bodily fluids from naturally harvested organs also requires periodic wiping of surfaces with a surfactant or bleach cleaner. Make sure to use a clean rag for this task rather than a sponge, as sponges grow germs quickly and cannot be thoroughly sanitized.

At this point, many of you are surely asking, "then what am I to DO with all of the organs and limbs in my home?" Rest assured, they may be discreetly and conveniently stored in your chest freezer in an airtight container or freezer safe bag. Large or oddly shaped pieces should be wrapped tightly in freezer paper for prolonged storage, though a trash bag can do for short-term. Proper wrapping and storage techniques will not only allow you to store exponentially more organs in a convenient, out of sight location, but will also ensure freshness for months to come.

For those who wish to display their organs, it is best to do so in a private space such as the bedroom or a library, provided the door may be closed when company arrives. Smaller organs may be stored in jars with preservatives. It can be difficult to find appropriately sized jars for larger organs, but the results are worth the trouble. Vacuum seal bags are another option that may serve you well.

Formaldehyde is an extremely useful preservative, but organs preserved chemically are, of course, not edible. Many homemakers prefer not to have harsh chemicals in the home as a matter of principle, preferring more natural methods. Some of my readers have reported success with pressure canning, vinegar, or salt packing, which I detailed in a series last year. Experiment with what works best for your own purposes.

The most traditional option is simply burying. Buried bodies have long been the best kept secret of any serious gardener. You too can "reap" these benefits! Just be sure to dig your hole deep enough to discourage scavengers, and the neighbors will turn green with envy, wondering what you have done to make your rhododendrons so lush. As always when gardening, be sure to wear a wide-brimmed hat to protect your complexion and quality gardening gloves to keep your nails free from grime and to protect your hands from calluses and keep them silky smooth.

Happy homemaking!

THE BUILD

"This is really going to be our home." Nate stares proudly at the empty lot. The glint of a tear in his eye makes me feel warm inside. We have worked so hard for this. Owning a home is a huge thing for any couple, but for Nate, this is the culmination of everything he ever wanted as a kid.

"It's all ours." I say, taking his hand."Yeah," he squeezes it and doesn't say anything else for a long time. He doesn't have to. I met him in college because we worked at the student center together. I always looked the other way when half eaten trays of pizza became fully eaten trays of pizza or when the crackers at the soup bar were particularly popular. I asked him out first, mainly because I wanted to see him eat a real meal. My roommates and I cooked for him at our apartment. He didn't know what to do with himself, but we ended up having a good time and decided to hang out again. And then we just never stopped until we both realized neither of us ever wanted to stop.

By that time I knew how he had grown up bouncing from apartment to apartment, couch to couch, sometimes staying with friends or relatives, sometimes staying places where his mother shushed him awake in the middle of the night and told him they had to leave right then. Sometimes his mother's car was the only thing that was between them and a Nor'easter.

At those times, she would keep a YMCA membership so they would have locker room access for hot showers and he would use the coffee table in the lobby to do his homework. It was really all he had to escape into, at least until he was old enough to use the weight room, so he got good at it. He got scholarships, took out some loans to cover the rest and a campus job at the student center.

"Our baby will never have to–" he can't finish. I pull him in and we hold each other there in the empty lot. I silently make a promise to him as I breathe in the smell of him. His warm arms envelop me, and I never want to leave. This home, this place, our family, forever, my heart whispers.

The plans are finalized. We made the decisions together, and there are a few things that were important to me, but this is Nate's house. I wanted it to be everything he'd ever hoped and prayed for, and his fingerprints are in everything, right down to the extra space for weight machines in the garage. Even with all of the moves and instability in his life, once he discovered weight lifting at the Y, he never gave it up. He's not the unnatural looking type of strong that you see on male models for kitschy birthday cards, with the six-pack and man-boob pecs, but he's the kind of built that makes you do a double take and think, "That dude probably works out a lot."

I'm more of a computer warrior. I use the dudes with man-boob pecs and six-packs as my avatars for RPGs. (I get fewer interactions with creeps that way.) A girl cave with some serious wifi was my main item on the wish list. I might do twinkle-lights in there if I'm feeling fancy.

Nate wants a big kitchen. I love that he wants a big kitchen. I don't cook anything more complicated than mac and cheese, but Nate has always wanted a big kitchen like in the cooking shows. "You'll never have to cook a thing. Just sit at the counter and keep me company while I figure out whatever the hell it means to spatchcock a chicken," he had said.

"Deal. What else are you bargaining for?"

"I don't know."

"Come on. I want to hear it. What's your wildest dream, Nate?"

He shakes his head. "It's kinda stupid."

"No cop outs. This is our Barbie Dream House, okay?"

He laughed. "I've never had my own Christmas tree."

My heart broke a little. I've learned a lot about his childhood in the years we've been together, but every now and then he pulls out a little punch to the gut like this one. Christmases at my parent's house are always magical. "We are ordering the biggest Christmas tree we can find and covering every inch of it in the tackiest ornaments possible."

"Where would all of that stuff even go?"

"That's what attics are for. And crawl spaces, if they are tall enough to be usable."

I will be filling every storage area I can find wall to wall with seasonal decor. I will be Martha flipping Stewart in the fall and full-on Clark Griswold at Christmas. Inflatable easter bunny? Why not? Fourth of July buntings? Sure. Giant skeletons in fairy costumes for Halloween. We can even throw in some random stuff like National Pancake Day flags and some Homestar Runner "Labor Daybor" tapestries in the in-between spaces.

I had already made my mind up before that night that I wanted to make sure he got a home that felt like it was truly his. We make good money between the two of us, but he's never owned more clothes than could fit in a duffel bag. Even in college, he knew he would change dorms every year and packed light. Never had his own Christmas tree.

I'm still musing on this when Nate startles me.

"Jumpy much?"

"No, I just didn't hear you come in."

"I'll make sure to talk to myself and bang into things next time."

"You do that."

"Should I break some dishes while I'm at it?" He asks as he gets a cereal bowl from the cabinet.

"No point. I know you're in here now."

"Oh, I know. I was asking for the next time."

"I see. Play it by ear then, I guess."

My phone dings an alert at work. I always forget to turn it on silent mode. Then when I turn silent mode on I forget to switch it back off and end up missing several days worth of calls and messages.

"Want to do something fun tonight?" the text reads.

"What do you have in mind?" I reply after I silence my notifications.

"A surprise."

"Should I be nervous?"

"That depends."

"On what?"

"What are your opinions on boiled calamari?" I snort. Pam from the cubicle across the aisle raises her eyebrows. I pass it off as a cough and reply.

"Extra tentacles?"

"Of course."

"Seriously though. Do I need to dress up or anything?"

"No. I got something for us. For the build."

"A life-sized Rick Astley cutout? It's a bit early."

"Richard Simmons"

"Also acceptable. I thought you said things were a little tight this month tho"

"The house made me do it."

"Well if you put it that way, it must be alright."

"Obviously. The house can do no wrong."

"Love u."

"<3"

Almost as soon as I get home Nate ushers me to his car. Giddiness is pouring off of him like a cup held under a waterfall. We get onto the highway out of town. When I see the exit he takes, I ask, "We're going out to the property?"

He shrugs. "It was lonely." We pull onto the lot and Nate goes to the back and takes something out of the trunk before I've even taken off my seatbelt. I shut the door and he brings it around to my side. He's holding a drone. It's not a massive, top of the line one, but nice enough that it can send a camera feed to his phone. This wasn't a Walmart special.

"Wow." It's actually pretty cool, but not something I've ever considered buying before.

"We can use it to watch the builders break ground next week."

"That's awesome," I say, and I mean it.

"I figure we can get some practice in now so that we won't drive it into an excavator or something."

"Probably a good idea."

Nate flies the drone around for a while then offers to let me have a turn. I'm decent at it. I've spent enough hours gaming with various consoles that a controller doesn't seem too strange to me.

"I'm good now." I hand the controller back and Nate continues flying it. It's spring, but it's still freezing out. I check my phone. We've been here for an hour.

"I'm getting cold, hon. Want to head home?" I ask.

"We are home." He smiles. I like the idea of watching the build from a cool perspective from time to time, but I'm pretty done.

"I guess I'll wait in the car then." I walk to the car and get in. I'm so cold that my muscles hurt from the involuntary clenching. It's still chilly in the car, but at least there's no wind in here and eventually I start to warm up.

I must have fallen asleep because it's dark when Nate gets into the car. The cold is bone deep.

"I can't see the build site in the dark," he says. I expect

more, an apology maybe, so I wait. But that's all he says. We ride home in silence.

The builders have begun framing and we can actually walk through our house and see the layout. Seeing a plan and seeing actual spaces with two by fours are worlds apart. I can start imagining where I am going to put things and how we will move through the living room and where the couch will sit.

I've made peace with making nearly daily trips to the house. I just remind myself of all the hope and love that Nate has poured into this dream of a forever home. Sometimes the way he talks, it's almost like the house is another living breathing family member. "Look at how you've grown!" he breathes before entering. I see his hands trace lines along the two by fours periodically as we tour the bare skeleton of what will someday be our home.

Nate bought a set of trail cameras. He's setting them up today all around the house. The strange thing is that he's not setting them from the house facing out. He's setting them up facing the house itself.

"Want to go to the house with me tonight after work?" Nate asks me over cereal.

"Why?" I ask.

"They are putting up drywall tomorrow and there's something I wanted to do there. Want to come?"

"No, not really." His eyebrows go up, in search of an explanation. "We've been almost every night for several weeks, and when we're there you completely ignore me. I just want to stay home."

Nate thinks for a while. "Are you jealous of the house?"

Yes. "What? It's not like that," I say, even though it sort of is.

"What is it then?" He asks calmly, but the question itself feels so out of touch with my reality that his calmness makes me question myself. I feel irrationally mad that he doesn't get this. That he needs an explanation at all. Hasn't he sensed my lack of enthusiasm on our nightly trips? Hasn't he felt us drifting away from each other? I take a deep breath and try to match his calm tone.

"We used to do things together, play games, visit family, hang out with friends. I feel like all we do lately is see what's new at the build site. I feel like I'm being ignored. I miss you. I miss us."

Nate pulls his chair next to mine and wraps his arms around me. God, I've missed this.

"I'm sorry," he whispers into my hair. Everything I've been feeling in the past weeks comes rushing out of me and suddenly I'm sobbing like a little kid. And it feels so good to feel him there with me that I don't try to stop. I'm afraid that if I do the spell will be broken and he will go back to the way things were. For now, right now, he's here, and he's mine.

Eventually my breathing evens out. I have a massive headache and Nate has to change his shirt because of all the snot and tears I've let run onto his shoulder.

We head to work and Nate texts me several times throughout the day. Nothing important. Just memes and sweet little "thinking of you," type things that make me feel warm and loved. When I get home he's already beaten me there.

"I have a surprise for you, if you'll trust me."

I want to trust him. I nod.

He leads me to his car. The back is full of stuff, including what looks like every blanket that we own. My heart sinks when I see that we are taking the familiar route to the build.

He senses my frustration, for once, and holds out his hand to me. "It will be different this time. Do you trust me?"

I take his hand. "Okay, but this had better be pretty good, whatever it is."

He looks hopeful and rubs the back of my thumb. It helps. We walk into the house, and I jump at the "Surprise!" that greets me. James and Twyla are there, and Sammie and Alexis. Nate has set up a card table and a space heater. The newly installed kitchen island, sans countertop, is covered with a length of board and laden with pizza boxes, two-liters, and chips.

We spend the evening laughing and eating. No one cares that the floor is covered in heavy paper or that there's dust and screws all around us. No one even cares that they have to excuse themselves to the port-a-potty because the plumbing isn't hooked up yet. We're just hanging out. In our home. And it's brilliant. Eventually James and Twyla say they are calling it a night and Sammie and Alexis get into their car.

When they drive off Nate grabs a bundle of blankets and a large bag and carries them into the house, to what will be our bedroom. He lays them out on the dusty, paper-covered floor and lays down. I lay next to him. It's not exactly comfortable on the hard floor, but I lean on his shoulder and feel closer to him than I have in weeks.

He kisses my forehead. Then my lips. I kiss him back. His hands wrap around my back and under my shirt. They are cold but getting warmer. We make love there on the saw-dusty concrete, in the pile made of every blanket we own.

It's cold. The bed is hard. I slowly come to the realization of where I am and that I've been asleep. And that I'm alone.

I can hear Nate walking around the house. He's muttering quietly and stopping at intervals along the walls, but it's too dark to make out what he's doing. I strain to hear him, but I can only catch a few words here and there.

"I know... working... don't have to... together..." Don't have to do what? I wonder, and who is he talking to? But I'm half asleep and nothing seems to make any sense. The next thing I know, Nate is in bed and the suggestion of a sunrise is filtering into the newly installed windows. His alarm is going off. He kisses me on the forehead.

"We'd better get the blankets back in the car before the workers start showing up," he says. I nod and suddenly hate my life when I sit up and pull the covers off, feeling stiff and cold from a night on the floor. Nate grabs the bundle, "I'll take first dibs on the port-a-potty if that's okay with you," he says. I can't help but smirk at the absurdity of that question as I nod. Nate walks out with the bundle.

The sun is coming in stronger now, and it occurs to me that I might be able to see what Nate was doing along the walls for so long last night while he's outside. I look around the walls trying to figure it out. At first I don't see anything, but then, what's that? The tiny white slivers, just a few, are placed in a small pile in a corner between framing boards. Fingernails? Now the cold is deeper than the temperature of the room.

I inspect the area further down the wall, going slowly, but I still almost miss it. A bit of tangled hair. I have the suspicion that it's mine, but I can't fathom why he would have put it there.

Nate has been staring at the camera feeds on his laptop

all day. They are remote accessible from his cell and computer and have night vision. He keeps a window up on a second monitor when he works from home. On Saturday he didn't even pretend to do anything but watch. It didn't even look like anyone was at the job site. Just an empty house.

I've tried not to judge. I've gotten some books about childhood trauma and I've tried to be understanding. I've been trying to get Nate to see a psychologist or a counselor.

"Why?" He asked when I brought it up again this morning. "I feel the happiest I've ever been. Like I've been asleep my whole life, or waiting maybe, and now the thing I've been waiting for is finally here. And we get to be together for this as a family. What else could I need?"

Something about that response lodged itself in the pit of my stomach like a lead pancake. It seems weird to be jealous of a house, but I feel like it's taken Nate from me. That he loves the house and the idea of us living together in it more than he actually loves me. I still can't make sense of my feelings about what's going on. All this time, I've been wondering if I am being unreasonable.

Something in me realizes that I simply can't do this. I can't continue watching the man I love refuse to get help, refuse to acknowledge that there's any problem here.

The house is nearly finished now. We arrive in the evening, just like we have done almost every day for months.

We get off work and come straight here. I never imagined working for something so hard only to resent it this much.

Nate goes around feeling the walls, muttering. I can't make out most of what he says but he's not saying it to me. Sometimes it sounds like a question. Like he's actually conversing with the house. I desperately want to know what is going on in his mind, but he's hardly talking to me anymore. He doesn't acknowledge that anything is wrong when it so obviously is. I cry myself to sleep. I wake up in the night and he's not in the room. I get up to see what he's doing up so late and stop in the doorway. He's sitting in the living room of our apartment watching the camera feeds to the house. He's talking to it again. He doesn't seem to know he's being watched, but I can't make out any of what he's saying. At this point, I'm not sure I want to.

We've gotten our certificate of occupancy. But I have not moved any of my things over. I should be elated to start moving in, but it feels wrong. Nate has been off the deep end for weeks, and I've come to a point where I've hit my limit. The level of crazy no longer hits me in surprising pangs. I'm living it twenty-four/seven so I just have a perpetual knot in my gut that tells me this can't go on any longer.

And it won't. Not for me anyway. I'm done. I have to be.

I pull into the drive feeling angry at the world for being so vibrant. The air is hot and humid, the trees in the fullness of their green. Cicadas scream from their branches, and I want to scream back at them. What I'm doing is the sort of thing that should be done on a cold, rainy day that looks as miserable as I feel. But the world doesn't give a shit about that.

"Nate?" I walk into the house, knowing he's here. I've come to say goodbye. I've loved Nate for ten years. That's not going to change anytime soon. This man may not be my Nate anymore, but I owe this to the man I loved. Still love. The man who used to love me. I will grieve later, I tell myself. Right now I just need to get this over with. I run my hands along the walls of the house that should have been my home trying not to imagine our unborn baby girl taking her first steps in this hall, Nate cheering her on with me as she reaches out to us. Hanging a painting in that corner. Watching movies snuggled together on a couch right there.

"I hear you. Yes. Okay. I get it." Nate's voice carries through the mostly unfurnished rooms. I walk into what should be our bedroom and find him facing the walls. "I was hoping to avoid it, but you're right, if it can't be helped I'll have to—"

"Nate." I interrupt him. "My stuff is packed at the apartment, but I'm not bringing it here." He turns, looking surprised to see me.

"You didn't tell me she was here now," he mutters.

My eyes sting, but I swallow the lump in my throat. "You seem disappointed to see me."

His face changes. He looks sorry. "Not disappointed,

27

just startled. What do you mean you aren't moving your things here?"

"I'm not moving into this house with you, Nate. There are a few things I need to figure out on my own. And there are some really big things you need to figure out on your own. But until then, I—" No. My voice can't break now. "I can't be a part of your life until then." There. I got the words out, and I didn't cry. I can cry later.

"No, no, no, no, no. Don't say that," Nate pleads. "Please, don't say that."   A breath leaves my chest in a huff. I am a torrent of emotion and suddenly anger surfaces. "Why not? You haven't listened to me asking you to get help for months. You talk to the house more than you talk to me. I don't get it!" I'm angry crying now and I hate it. It makes my words hard to understand and I always feel like a child when I do it. Like nothing I say will be interpreted as rational. Behold exhibit A, hysterical female. But I press on. "Why won't you get help? Where did you go?"

"I'm right here." He looks so hurt. I want to hug him and tell him I didn't mean it. But I do mean it. I have to mean it. I can't waver. I can't let this, whatever it is, swallow me up.

"Unless you fix things, if you're here, then I can't be." I wipe my nose with my sleeve. Willing myself to just turn around and walk away, but feeling like my feet are tethered to the spot.

"But the house, I mean the baby— Where will you go?"

28

"I'll let you know when I figure it out."

"I KNOW!!!" He shouts it, but not at me. It's as though there's another person in the room interrupting in the most egregious way. "Sorry, just, please, don't do this. Don't leave. I know I've been shit. But please, you don't understand. We have to be together. We have to."

"I don't understand? I understand that nothing has been the same between us since we started building this house. I hate it. I hate what it's done to us."

Nate's jaw tightens and his eyes go wide. "Don't say that," he says in a stern whisper. The kind I used to get in church when my mom was about to drag me out and spank me in the parking lot. But he doesn't look angry — more, I don't know — scared? "I know it's been hard, hon, but the house just wants us to be together. I want us to be together. Here. Please?" The panic and sadness is bubbling closer and closer to the surface, and I can't stand to look at him anymore. It hurts too much. Finish now, grieve later, I tell myself again.

God, I love him so much, and my heart is breaking. "I have to go."

I turn and walk away. It's done. I did it.

My shoulder slams into the garage door. Nate is on me. Pressing me against it. My protruding belly keeps me from facing completely forward. He's crying. "It wasn't enough. I tried so hard, but it wasn't ever going to be enough. I'm so sorry." His body pins mine and I hear him pull tape from a roll. He begins wrapping my hands behind me.

"What are you doing, Nate?"

"We have to be together. You, me and the baby. The house wants us to be together." He gently pulls the hair back from my eyes and kisses my cheek. "You have to stay. You just have to."

"Let me go, Nate. Please. This isn't funny."

"No, it's not. I'm so sorry. I don't know how to explain it, but you can't go. Can't you feel it?"

"Feel what?" I should be fighting, but this is the most open Nate has been in weeks and I can't help but be curious. Besides that, I'm pretty sure my fight, flight or freeze reaction has always been set to freeze mode.

"The house. Can you feel it? Can you hear it?"

"I don't know what you mean."

"It wants us to be happy. It wants us to be together. You can't go, and I can't let you. I'm so sorry."

It's never crossed my mind until now that Nate would ever, could ever, hurt me. Even when he was talking to the walls I still felt like I could trust him on that level. But with my hands duct taped behind my back and Nate pinning me to the wall, I can't think of anything beyond what he could do to me if he wanted to. I'm completely at his mercy and I can't do a damn thing about it.

He kicks my feet together and I almost lose my balance. He squats and holds my legs together, wrapping them in more layers of duct tape. He drops the roll on the floor and scoops me into his arms, giving a little toss to better distribute my weight.

"Time to carry the bride over the threshold," he says with a grim smile. He carries me back to the bedroom and places me on the bare mattress that was delivered earlier this week, still wrapped in plastic.

He leaves the room, but returns a moment later, the roll of duct tape in hand. He runs so many layers over me that the roll nearly empties.

"Now we can be together," he says.

"This isn't being together, Nate. This is kidnapping. You have to let me go. Plcase, Nate."

"I can't. The house isn't right without you. We love you. You don't know it now, but you will soon. I'll let you get some rest." He kisses the top of my head, the gesture so sweet and gentle, it would have given me butterflies on any other day. Today it makes me try to cringe away from him to wonder how twisted his idea of love is that he could do this. He closes the door gently as he leaves the room.

I try to wriggle out of the duct tape, but there are so many layers, I'm not going anywhere. I keep trying, but the duct tape pulls at my skin and the multiple layers keep it from tearing. Exhausted, eventually the only thing left for me to do is dwell on my fear, the irritated skin from the tape, the itching stream of snot and tears on my face that I can't wipe away, the pins and needles in my arms, and threading through all of it, my shock and pain in the fact that Nate could do this. If he could do this, what else might he be capable of? I'm carried off in a maelstrom of feelings, helplessly tossed by vortex into my own memories and imaginings until I succumb to its current and can't think anymore.

It's dark when I wake up. I don't know where I am. The events from the day play through my head, but I'm not strapped to a bed anymore. The duct tape is gone. The abrasions on my wrists and ankles still sting, though. Whatever is underneath me is not covered in crinkly mattress warehouse plastic, but a layer of something dry and loose. Dirt, I think. I reach out, trying to make sense of my surroundings. My hand meets a hard, rough surface. I find rectangular tracks along it. Mortar. Cinder blocks. On all sides.

Panic starts to rise. I sit up and reach around me, above me, trying to find some sort of opening, some door or window. The cinderblock perimeter is solid and I find that I am lucky to not be an inch or two taller or my head would have hit the ceiling when I sat up.

Breathing hard and fast, I will myself to stay calm. If this is our crawlspace, there's no way Nate would have had the time or know-how to Cask of Amontillado me properly. Maybe I can bust out before everything sets. Slower. Slower. Breathe. Okay.

I turn my body to the right. There's just enough room for me to coil my body up for a good kick. No give. Again. Nothing. Another. Another. Another. I lose count. I lose my breath. I give one last long shove, bracing my back on the opposite wall. I scoot down and try another spot. And another. The walls are solid. I try scratching at the mortar with my fingernails looking for weak places where it might not be set where I could just maybe scratch enough mortar out to loosen a block. I trace each line around and up and down. I found the weak spot. My fingers. The tips are raw and the nails feel chewed to bits, but I can't stop looking, checking again and again. I bang on the ceiling.

It bangs back. It's muffled, but it's near. Whatever is making the noise. Maybe someone came over. I hit the ceiling as hard as I can. My fists protest against this abuse as I stop to listen for a response. "CAN YOU HEAR ME?" I yell. "IS SOMEONE THERE?"

I listen and I hear someone as though from many rooms away. It's a whisper in me ear, but they are shouting. He is. Nate.

"Where is she?" A pause. "What do you mean, 'she's safe?' We're supposed to be together, why are you keeping her from me? Lexie! Can you hear me? Where are you?" His voice becomes clearer in my ear as I listen for it. He sounds frantic, like someone else moved me. I would think that maybe they were moving me to protect me from him, but then why the walls? If Nate didn't do this— but of course he did. Who else

33

could it have been? Maybe he's regretting his choices, dissociating in some way and can't remember what he's done. If he's lucid for now, maybe I should risk it.

"I'M HERE! IN THE CRAWLSPACE!"

"LEXIE!" He's heard me.

"NATE, LET ME OUT! I'M IN THE CRAWLSPACE!"

"LEXIE, IF YOU CAN HEAR ME LET ME KNOW WHERE YOU ARE!"

"I'M RIGHT HERE!!!" I'm screaming. "I'M RIGHT HERE, CAN'T YOU HEAR ME?"

"This is not okay. You have to let me know where she is, or swear to God, I will get a sledgehammer and knock down every goddamned wall."

"NATE, I'M HERE! PLEASE!" My words are devolving into sobs, but I have to make him hear me. "I'M HERE, NATE! "WHY CAN'T YOU HEAR ME?"

I woke up in the dark for the third time just now. It doesn't feel as dark now though. Sometimes it almost feels as though I can start to see around me, just a little bit. The thought crosses my mind that I haven't eaten or drank anything in, if I had to guess, maybe a couple of days. I haven't needed to go to the bathroom either. Is this what dying of dehydration is like? Surely not. But logically, it doesn't make sense. What I can see of my bloody fingers and raw wrists and ankles look worse than I would have thought, but they don't particularly bother me. I'm just here. In the dark.

It's kind of restful actually. Quiet. Calm. The dirt at my back feels soft. I've accepted that I'm not getting out of here. I'm probably going to die here. Sometimes, in the last day or maybe more, I've heard Nate calling for me. I've heard crashes and crumbles, like he's making good on his promise to tear up the house. But he's not been able to hear me. I've given up on that. I just listen. And wait. And then things get quiet again for a while.

My belly feels a little tighter than I'm used to. A bit like cramps or constipation. Maybe the no bathroom thing is finally catching up with me. I'm not exactly sure what to do in such close quarters. Use the corner I guess. I scoot as far as I can to the end of my little room and bear down. Nothing happens. I try again and again. A pain coming in waves, but somehow dulled. This isn't a bowel movement.

The baby is coming. A part of me knows that this is so fucking tragic. This child is going to die here with me, if we even both survive the birth. But there's nothing I can do, and I feel distant to the pain. Like part of me is elsewhere, watching events unfold on a low budget movie. Blood is everywhere, but the strange thing is that the more of it there is, the better I can see my surroundings. There's not much to see beyond a whole lot of blood though. It mixes with the dirt floor beneath me making a gruesome slurry as I shift and strain. Is this the normal amount of blood?

I feel a great shift as I push and I sense the pain from miles away as it subsides. I'm cold and exhausted. My whole body aches from shivering. I'm floating. A bit of vertigo. Falling? Nauseous. Tired. My eyes close for a blink. A longer blink.

I wake up with a start, I don't know how much later. There's still no light source here in the walled-off crawlspace, but I can see around me as though the light is being emanated from the walls and things around me. It's silent.

A panic crosses my mind and I reach down between my legs. Surely a baby would be crying and cold. I don't want to look, to see the object of so many hopes and dreams, the flesh of my body. But I have to know. Is she... I can't stop myself. It's not a pretty sight, but it's also the most beautiful sight I've ever seen. The baby, my baby, is covered in various layers of goo that are coagulating. I love her so much, have waited for her for so long. Her eyes are closed and I hold my breath. Her body doesn't feel warm when I pick her up. So light, so tiny, so perfect, and my breath waits. She nuzzles toward me, and I sigh in relief. I hold her to my breast, she takes it but does not swallow. She is peaceful, calm, this bone of my bone and flesh of my flesh. Wherever she is, I will be. Taigh, the Scottish Gaelic word for house. She is my Home, my family. I am Home.

I want to clean Taigh, to wrap her in warm things. I touch the wall and my hand passes through it, allowing me in like an embrace. I feel the House. I hear it whispering to me its hopes and joys and a sense of peace passes through me as I pass through the wall that has made itself a door to me. I know that Nate loves her too. I can't explain it, but I can feel his love now, like it's part of the house itself as much as any two by four or ceiling joist, part of my own thoughts as I pass through it. It's so glad we're here.

I wash Taigh in the bathroom and find some blankets. Then we live. Together.

Time passes, but I don't care how much. We don't seem to need to eat. Sometimes we sleep though. Taigh stays tiny but never cries. She is the sweetest baby, all nuzzles and snuggles. I could sit and hold her forever.   Sometimes people come by but we don't pay them much attention until one day a young couple comes in with a lady in a skirt suit. The couple are young and hopeful. They don't seem to notice us, but we can feel their dreams like sunshine, their love for each other, their love for the House. We love them too, House, Taigh and me. We want them to stay forever.

"What do you think, Hon?" the man says. "Is this our forever home?"

She smiles. "I think so."

-2-

BATHROOMS

Adventures in Bathroom-ing

Elsie Munroe

While bathrooms are a necessity in a home, they are often neglected as an environment in which we live. Bathrooms should be an inviting space, well organized, and above all, clean.

Take care that each bathroom in the home should be equipped with its own toilet brush and plunger. "Why not just one for the household," you ask? Put yourself in the place of a guest. Imagine that you have just lost four pounds in the space of three minutes and the plumbing seems inadequate to the task. Would you feel comfortable returning to the drawing room in the presence of the other guests to inquire as to the location of a plunger?

Ensuring that every bathroom is equipped is ensuring that every bathroom guest is equipped. Likewise, make sure that other necessities are in a well organized and easy to find location, including towels, wash cloths, extra bathroom tissue rolls, and poisons.

When someone decides that it's Uncle Henry's time to go, who are you to disagree with a guest? Be a considerate host. Make sure your guests do not have to go through the embarrassment of inquiring after the bathroom supplies they need.

Happy homemaking!

Michal Leigh

Callus Removal

I know this looks bad, but let me explain. You see, I had a callus on my big toe that had been bothering me for a while. It seemed a little thick to try to file away. So I grabbed the clippers and took a few pieces off. But I didn't feel anything and it was obvious that I wasn't anywhere near anything important, so I cut a bit deeper. No blood, nothing but leathery old skin. So I went a bit deeper. Same thing. Again and again I cut away bit by bit bound by some morbid curiosity of how far it would go. In this manner, I removed the first inch of my toe. At this point I abandoned the clippers and experimented. A garden lopper took the rest of the toe with no pain, no blood, only uniformly dense, white skin. I went up incrementally from there, until the width of my leg proved too much. By now I was driven by compulsion. Come what may, I had to know where it ended. So I grabbed the chainsaw. Both legs, same. My torso, same.

Once I'd taken the left arm at the shoulder, I could hardly do the right. So... Do you think you could help me out?

Foot Cream

Gerald fell flat on his face. It was too much. The weight of it all. He didn't know how anyone could stand it. His shoulders began to shake, and his breath came out in heaving sobs. The children starving in war-torn countries stared at him from behind his tears. Commercials of sad puppies between late night reruns. Every homeless person he had ever driven by, pretending not to notice. Every insult he'd given without stopping to wonder if he had been the one in the wrong.

But there was beauty too. The delicate petals of a violet on a May lawn. The soft look on his wife's face when she sidled up beside him on the couch. The world was beautiful and horrific and sharp, and just too much to contain.

That's where Dorris found him, on the sheet vinyl floor next to the commode, paralyzed with wonder and ecstasy and despair.

"Gerald!"

He gave no response. He couldn't. Dorris's eyes fell on something small and white at Geralds feet. An open tube with a blue label. Her eyes weren't as good as they used to be. She lifted the small white tube with shaking hands, wondering if Gerald had somehow managed to poison himself.

It looked like a new brand of foot cream. Surely that couldn't poison Gerald, but still. Something was terribly wrong. She got onto the tablet their daughter had given them to find the number for poison control. Perhaps he had gotten mixed up and ingested it. She dialed the number on her phone.

"Poison control center," came the female voice on the other end.

"It's my husband," Dorris answered numbly.

"What seems to be the issue, ma'am?"

Dorris carefully explained Geralds symptoms and described the tube she'd found.

"I see. Seems like an overdose. You'll need to wash off the excess cream, but he should be okay in a few hours without further intervention."

"Overdosed on a foot cream? You don't think he's gone funny and eaten it, do you?"

"No ma'am. It's actually a pretty common mistake."

"Mistake?"

"Yes. Just to be sure, go ahead and read the full label."

That would be a problem. Dorris took several deep breaths and tried to tell herself everything was going to be alright. She had to get her hands to stop shaking. And her readers. She'd never be able to see the fine print otherwise.

"Ma'am?"

"Yes. I just need my readers. I can't read a thing without them." Dorris took the tube with her, reluctantly leaving her quivering husband's side again to retrieve her readers from the bedside table. She had to shuffle through a pile of books that she was reading, an assortment of Important Papers that tended to collect there, and a tangle of charging cords before she found them. She read aloud, "Callous Remover."

"Okay, can you read the back for me as well, ma'am?"

"Sure. It says, 'For the removal of stubborn callouses. Use as recommended.'"

"Keep going."

Dorris did.

"'Apply a small drop, roughly the size of a pea, to a fingertip. Rub on chest. Wash hands thoroughly after use.' Why would you put a foot cream on your chest?"

"A little further."

Dorris kept on. "'Use sparingly. Potential side effects include, but are not limited to existential crises, intense feelings of guilt and/or euphoria, and extreme empathy and irrational behavior, which may include uncontrollable laughing or crying and irrational behavior. Do not make financial decisions within five hours of dose.'"

"That's what I thought. Spell out the label for me."

"C-A-L-L-O-U-S."

"Yes. That spelling is important, but these products are easily confused. Your husband bought the wrong cream. Just wipe it off with a damp wash rag and some soap if you can't get him into the bath, and—"

The woman's voice faded away.

Dorris set the phone down, considering Gerald. Extreme empathy? She loved Gerald, but the most personal gift he'd given her in the last twenty years was a new vacuum cleaner. Perhaps this wasn't such a bad thing. Still, he wasn't used to it. He'd better not endure it alone. Dorris placed a pea sized drop of ointment on her finger and applied it to her chest as directed. She washed her hands carefully at the sink and wrapped her arms around the man she married, cradling him like a child until they fell asleep in each others' arms.

The Importance of Drain-Care

Harry had never seen light before. It had heard the Voices talking to each other though. Sometimes they sounded kind. Sometimes they sounded angry. Gradually Harry came to understand them to some degree. On the day that he first saw true light, it had heard them talking about something called a drain. One Voice, the one called James, was asking the other Voice called Sarah to clean it out.

"The shower's hardly draining. It's not my hair in there. I'm not doing it anymore," he said.

"Fine," Sarah had said. Though it did not truly sound like it was. "I'll put it on my list of other crap I have to do."

Then the Voices argued for a while, and then things were quiet for a time, and then Harry's life was forever changed. He felt a tugging and a ripping. He was sure he was going to be torn apart, he felt himself stretching until finally something gave way and he was loose. And there it was. Light. Dazzling, brilliant light. And the first and most beautiful thing he had ever seen.

"Oh my god!" This beautiful thing was the Sarah-voice. "I'm pretty sure this thing has been down there so long it's become sentient. Come check it out!"

"Why on earth would I want to do that?" came the James-voice.

"Because I think I just saw it move!"

The James-thing entered the room, and Harry saw what it looked like as it said, "Ugh, that's so gross. I really don't know why I came in here."

"To help me give it a name."

"You are so fucking weird."

"You know you want to." Sarah dangled it closer and closer to James's face.

"Get that thing away from me!"

"It's just hair."

"And slime," he added.

"Okay, and slime, but mostly hair."

"Fine, call it Harry, can we please throw it away now?"

"Okay, spoilsport," Sarah laughed.

"Whatever."

48

Harry was unceremoniously tossed into a bin lined with a crinkly bag. The James and the Sarah were gone. It was strange and dry here. Harry didn't yet know the word for it, but it felt naked in the openness of the trash bin. Then Harry did something it had never done before. Almost without realizing the cause, Harry found itself in a new position. It had moved.

Before, in its pipe, Harry had merely existed in the darkness of its pipe. The pipe had seemed the right size because Harry had never known anything different. But even as its outer layers of conditioner, soap scum, epithelial cells and mucus protested this hostile atmosphere, Harry knew that it was now experiencing something that it hadn't realized had been missing from its existence thus far. Movement. Self determination.

Freedom.

Harry's slime stuck to the plastic bin liner, and with much time and effort it rolled its way to the top. A universe awaited. Harry did not have eyes, much less tear ducts, but if it had, it would have cried at the awe-inspiring expanse it sensed in the wide, open bathroom. There have been a few paradigm altering experiences that have changed the world forever. The reunion of the East and West hemispheres. Neil Armstrong's "giant leap for mankind." Harry knew nothing of these, and yet he knew something of their weight in its own globby little way.

The pipe could never be Harry's home again.

Harry felt the promise of new horizons stretching out before it. It felt the beauty and the wonder of the unknown. It felt the itch to explore. Even as it mourned the loss of something that it had been and could never be again.

Home.

Having seen, or rather, sensed all of this, Harry could never relegate itself back to its meager existence in the pipe. In its whirlwind of emotion, Harry made a decision. A small step. A giant leap. Harry splatted onto the floor and began to roll, its flagella making smacks upon the tile that were imperceptible to the James and the Sarah that, unbeknownst to Harry, were in the next room.

Harry found dust behind the toilet. There were some delicious spores growing in the caulking along the base of the tub. Harry hungrily absorbed all that it could.

Though Harry remembered a time when the bathroom was an unimaginable expanse, the time came when Harry felt that it had explored everything there was to explore there. Everything but one.

There was a darkness. A horizontal crack in the bathroom universe that lead to... something? Maybe nothing. Maybe the universe ceased to exist there. Maybe it was a tiny space where Harry would become trapped and spend its existence in darkness and monotony, made hell by the knowledge that things other than monotony existed.

Harry made another few patrols of the bathroom, but it kept coming back to the dark gap along the edge of the door. Finally, Harry could stand it no longer. If it didn't find out what was beyond that darkness, Harry might as well go back to the pipe. It needed to learn. It had to.

Harry emerged on the other side of the door onto a plush carpet. The fibers irritated Harry, though it wasn't sure why. They prickled and made movement harder. Harry felt pain for the first time. Harry set this aside and tried to make sense of its surroundings. The bathroom had been expansive, but this room...

Harry had no idea such things could exist, even after discovering the bathroom. A noise caught Harry's attention. It was a sort of snuffly, gurgling sound, similar to the sound the pipes made as a drain emptied. It was coming from a raised platform in the center of the room.

Harry felt very small and very old. It worked its way across the carpet. Harry used the last of its strength to climb the fabric draped off of the platform, only to find that the source of the noise was none other than the James and the Sarah.

A rush of nostalgia flooded through Harry. It was grateful to the James and the Sarah for giving it a new life and enabling it to see all sorts of wonders. But Harry felt tired, so, so tired. And dry. Of all the things in the universe, here at the end, Harry wanted to be close to the James and the Sarah. Harry wanted to visit its pipe one last time.

The noise issued again from the James's mouth. It was wide open. It was dark, and damp. It was close to one whom

Harry owed everything. It was everything its pipe had ever been and more. It was peace.

With what Harry knew would be its last effort, it rolled up the bed, up the warm face of the snoring James.

Harry had had a good existence.

Harry took a leap just as it took the greatest leap of all into the unknown from which there can be no return. Harry died exactly where it wanted to.

James sat up coughing.

"Mphg," the Sarah groaned.

"What the fuck?" The James asked when he'd finally stopped coughing. "Sarah?"

"Mmm?" The Sarah was not really awake.

"Did you—?"

The Sarah snored. The James concluded that she probably hadn't. He got up, carried the nasty wad of hair to the trash, peed, made an obligatory pass of his hands under the tap, and went back to bed.

"Always assemble necessary ingredients before starting a recipe for a more enjoyable cooking experience."

Elsie Munroe

-3-
KITCHENS

The Heart of the Home

Elsie Munroe

There is no place that holds more happy memories in the home than its kitchen. I treasure the memories I have of cutting out cookies with my grandmother at her big, oak kitchen table, as I listened to her stories of the old country and her warbling songs that felt as ancient as time itself.

At home the chrome and formica table was everything to me. It was a place to share about my day. A place where empty bellies were filled. A few pillows and king sized sheets made it a club house. It was also the place where my mother and my grandmother taught me to taste after additions of this and that in order to learn the magic of spices.

My mother was a marvel of feminine accomplishment. I will always remember the way she served my father. She wore her pearls and pumps, looking every bit the domestic goddess that I'd seen in the Sears and Roebuck advertisements for beautiful electric range ovens with sleek lines and black and white tile floors. She said the roast was a very special family recipe and that she would teach it to me someday.

Of course we missed him from time to time, but it was such a memorable meal that I looked forward to the day I could prepare a similar meal when I grew up. The years passed, and shortly before my wedding, my mother approached me and asked if I wanted to learn the family secret to the extra special roast, and did I ever!

I hope I don't anger my foremothers in their graves by sharing it with you now. You see, the secret to a truly delicious roast lies in a few key things. For one, the beast is better when largely sedentary. For another, a the volume of a roast necessitates more seasonings than most intrepid homemakers

are willing to apply. Rosemary is always a
valuable addition, as are garlic and onion, but
a proper amount of salt is essential. This can
be tweaked in the later stages of cooking if
you are afraid of overdoing it. But the most
important factor in creating a roast that
people will remember for years to come is
that you don't actually roast it at all!

Roasting is a dry preparation wherein
the meat is left uncovered. This often leads to
lackluster results where the best of cuts can
end up dry and tough. The best roast is
actually BRAISED! Braising is when the food
is allowed to cook slowly in its own juices or
in added liquids. This results in a meat that is
tender beyond compare. It does require more
time to develop an attractive level of
browning this way, but this is in exchange for
a reduced chance of burning a prime cut of
meat and the results are well worth the extra
time — time which could easily be spent on
other household tasks, or dare I say, enjoying
a tipple to celebrate your efforts in the
kitchen. This technique can be applied to
pork roasts, beef roasts, and even chicken.

I need to get ready now. My dress is
pressed, my reddest of red lipstick is waiting,

My highest of high heels are polished, and my pearls are already donned for my husband who is looking forward to an extra special meal tonight. I haven't given him any details yet. Won't he be surprised! Wish me luck, and as always, happy home-making!

The Disposal

I have a complicated relationship with my garbage disposal. I love that I don't have to pick all of the gross bits out of a little strainer all of the time. That in itself makes it worth owning one. I'm pretty sure.

I'd never had one until I lived in an apartment in college. I didn't really get the point of one right away. My roommate kept leaving bowls half full of food, popcorn hulls and other crap in the sink. I dumped them in the trash. She said that was what the disposal was for. Interesting that, seeing as I don't think she ever actually used it. I never really did either when I was cleaning up after her. It just seemed a bit scary. And once a spoon got caught in it. The noise was like physical pain, the aural equivalent of holding an electric fence for as long as you can.

On the other hand having a disposal was damn near indispensable when I was pregnant. Hyperemesis is a hell of a thing. I lost twenty pounds the first trimester. Couldn't keep a damn thing down. And of course the only things that sounded good were shit or contraband. Stuff I don't even like most days. I wanted coffee. Gallons of margaritas. Hot sauce by the bowlful. Buckets of fried chicken so greasy they practically float. I ate yogurt, bananas, and saltines. They came up anyway. I wonder if it was the kid being contrary against the "DO NOT EAT WHILE PREGGO" list or if it was me all along.

I looked like a tootsie pop if the sucker had managed to fall halfway down the stick. Constantly exhausted, I actually had a fender bender because I fell asleep at a red light and let off the brake. I became closely intimate with every form of vomiting. The way most of it would soak into grass except the chunky bits. The way it would hit the water in the toilet bowl with such force that I worried about ingesting toilet water from the backsplash. Once, when I didn't have enough warning to do anything to prevent it, I learned how effectively it clogged the drainpipe of the bathroom sink. Greg– that's my husband– had to take the pipe off to unclog it. The man was a goddamn saint that day.

I tell you my life changed when I discovered the glorious luxury of vomiting multiple times a day into a garbage disposal. There is zero backsplash. There is clean drinkable water that you can use to swish between projections. No mess to clean up. I fucking loved that thing.

Hard to believe that I used to think it was scary. It's ability to simply make things disappear is incredible. Doing the dishes, a stray bit of chicken bone went down and it didn't miss a beat. It just kept grinding and grinding and grinding, and with plenty of water and ice cubes it was gone just as entirely as if I had magicked it away to another dimension. The tiny bit of bone washed down to the sewage pipes and so forth could be anywhere or nowhere at all.

The thought came unbidden of the disposal sucking up my arm to the elbow. The thought sent a shiver down my spine, of fear, yes, but also exhilaration. Was it strong enough? I knew that my husband had installed the strongest model that could be purchased at our local hardware store. He didn't believe in doing things by halves. Neither did I, but I was methodical, testing the waters so to speak.

First I tried a carrot. It shivered as the blades ground it into oblivion. Water and ice. The carrot had never existed. Something that had been, no longer was. Stripped down to parts, components, motes peacefully floating in water. I imagined them to be little more than atoms.

That was the first night I dreamed about it, the disposal. Disappearing into eternity, floating away. Things that were, in the process of unraveling, un-becoming, un-being.

The next day I tried more bits and bobs from the fridge. The disposal seemed so hungry. Like it wanted more. I did what I could, and it whispered to me in my thoughts and in my dreams. Give me life, it said. Give me food. Give me blood.

The thought startled me. My hand slipped on the knife I

was using. Of course it was an accident. But there it was. Deep rubies welling up along a small nick in my finger. I couldn't let it go to waste when I could almost hear it calling to me. Life. Give me life.

I pressed the base of my finger and ran it down the length toward the cut, working a few drops into the white porcelain sink. The red was brighter now, imperfect circles that turned pink as I turned on the water and flipped the switch. I suppose I didn't really need to run the disposal in order for a few drops of blood to go down the drain. But it seemed right. I could tell that's what the disposal wanted, to chew. To grind. To devour Life.

I went upstairs and bandaged my finger. That's when the contractions started. Suffice it to say, that an eventful couple of days ensued and then Greg and I came home with Gabrielle, all eight pounds, three ounces of her.

The first few days home were a fog. I vaguely remember wetting myself a few times. I mostly slept. I nursed. I changed diapers. But mostly I slept. Although sleep isn't exactly the right term for it. I watched. Semiconscious. This beautiful, fragile life that I had knit together somehow. I watched how her body breathed marveling that I had no control over this process. That this body that had so recently been a part of my body, no longer was, and I couldn't will it to breathe. It happened of its own accord. I was in awe. Would she stop breathing? What could I do about it if she did? She was mine and yet not a part of me and yet still a part of me, but I had no control over this thing, this person, who was not me, but had been.

Hobbling the distance to the bathroom gradually became easier and I began to make it there in time more often than not. Eventually I resumed a few normal household duties. Mainly cooking meals. That's when the dreams started again. Water swirling the kitchen drain, whirring, grinding, blood. Life. Give me Life.

Gabrielle did keep breathing. She smiled her first smile. She pooped and peed and stared into space with a bewildered expression. She cried and slept. Over time my paranoia, the constant watching for the rise and fall of her chest, faded to be replaced with the first delicate shoots of attachment. I was allowed to love her. I allowed myself to accept her reality and to hope for her permanence in our family as the dangers of SIDS became less probable.

Every day I felt the pull, a whispering voice in the back of my mind. Life. Give me Life. I swept and mopped. I took out trash. And one day, I found a mouse in a trap in the garage. When I was that it was still alive, the whisper became an insistent shout. LIFE! GIVE ME LIFE!

It rang in my ears even though none could hear it but me. The screaming vibrated through my body. I could sense its hunger, its need. I could feel it reverberating, echoing off the walls within my skull. Intensifying. It hurt. Too much. I had to stop. Had to make it stop. I fed the mouse to the disposal.

That was the first living thing that I fed to the disposal. I threw up afterward and fed that to the disposal too. But it knew how to get its way now. It wasn't going to be satisfied with one meal.

It threw tantrums that reverberated in my brain with greater and greater frequency. At first I staved them off with bugs, worms, things I could find easily. But it was never enough. I resisted in my own way.

My skin crawled. So I scratched until it bled. My dreams disturbed, yet fascinated me in a way I found terrifying. So I stayed awake. Where was Greg?   Well, my leave was unpaid. Of course Greg had taken a couple of weeks, but we really couldn't afford more. So once I was able to walk from one end of the house to the other without peeing blood on the floor, we agreed that he should go back to work. Gabrielle and I saw him in the evenings. He helped. He changed diapers. He loved us. But he's never been the particularly observant type when it comes to anything beyond the surface. And given what I was dealing with, I didn't have the words to describe it. Not without sounding crazy, that is.

Sleep starved and jaw clenched and aching, I found myself I strapping Gabrielle into her car seat and driving to the pet store. I didn't really know what people did at pet stores. I'd never had one, but I knew what I was there for. I wandered around for a while, for form's sake. It seemed that was what the other customers were doing. I scoped out the cages for anything that I could morally justify feeding to the disposal.

The feeder mice with their unnaturally pink eyes somehow seemed less tragic to feed to the disposal than a little brown mouse. They were meant as livestock, nothing more. I'd never been a vegetarian. This was essentially tiny cows. Dumber. Uglier. Bred for food.   I kept them in a plastic box I drilled a hole in. I hid it from Greg by burying it behind the stacks of too big toddler clothes people gifted us at baby showers in Gabrielle's closet. He hardly went in there anyway.

The peace that followed each feeding became my only relief. Then it became a fixation. Then an addiction. It's not so much that it felt good to feed the disposal, as that every day that I didn't felt more and more like hell. Greg started to notice.

"Gabby keep you up last night?" Greg asked me over his Cheerios.

"What? Oh. I mean, Yeah. It was rough." She hadn't.

"That's so weird that I don't even hear her when she wakes up."

I wish I had that luxury. "I could wake you."

"If you need to, I suppose, but I'm not really equipped to feed her. There's no sense in us both being tired. I mean, unless you want to switch to formula for night feedings or pump of something."

"No. I don't want to do that."

" I figured, but I just want you to know that it's okay if

you change you mind, you know? You don't have to prove anything."

I had everything to prove. All the time. All moms do. Two seconds away and baby gets hurt. Too long between changes and baby gets a rash. Too much of this, too little of that, and a tiny person fucking dies. How does one person end up with the brunt of that responsibility? "I get it."

"Do you? Because you look like an extra from a zombie movie."

"Gee, thanks."

He rolled his eyes. "You know what I mean."

" Yeah? Tell me anyway," I challenged.

"I just mean that you don't have to do it perfectly. You don't have to do all of the things and be all the things all the time."

From where I stood, that was a baldfaced lie. I could see the judgement, from my mom, the church ladies, from myself, felt it wrapping around everything I did cinching me tighter with every exhalation until there would be no more give. Every morning I still approached the crib with that tightness in my chest until I could see with my own eyes the rise and fall of Gabrielle's tiny one. Seeing her blue and limp until the second my eyes confirmed her to be pink and wiggling. Almost every mom in the history of momming had somehow managed, one way or another. I nodded. "I'll be fine."

Greg offered to call in. I told him to not be ridiculous and promised to catch an extra nap and make sure to eat and drink at regular intervals.

Once Gabrielle was down for a nap I tried to keep my promise. I shoved something down my throat from the fridge, I don't remember what, and laid down on the couch.

Blood. So much blood. Screaming. Grinding almost inaudible from the screams. Until there wasn't any more. I woke up sobbing, covered in sweat. Gabrielle was crying and I couldn't soothe her. My wracking sobs made me incapable of it. I just held her as we both screamed, both needing to know that we weren't alone, that the other still existed.

That night while Greg was asleep I took a wrench to the disposal. I ripped it off the sink and the drain and tore our the wires. I wiped up the mess and threw a bucket under the sink. Greg came in just as I threw it in the garage trash bin.

"What are you doing up? It's like two in the morning."

"I know. I was just heading to bed."

That night I slept soundly for the first time in months. I was so sleep deprived that I must have slept in, and by some miracle Gabrielle had too. I woke up to grunting and clanging from downstairs. After checking to make sure Gabrielle was still breathing, I walked into the kitchen to find Greg on the floor, half under the sink cabinet. He'd just finished reinstalling the garbage disposal.

"What the heck were you doing last night?"

I couldn't breathe. Couldn't speak. Couldn't cry. How do you even begin to explain that your kitchen appliance wants to eat your baby? I shook my head.

"I'm worried, Jess. You haven't been yourself in weeks. What do you need?" He looked at me pleadingly but I didn't know where to begin. "Please tell me. Whatever it is. I just want to help."

Rip out the disposal. Please rip out the disposal. Smash it with a hammer, and tear it into pieces LIFE! haul it out to the curb, and GIVE ME LIFE! make sure that it never comes back, and— "Let's just get out of the house today," I heard myself say.

"Anywhere in particular?"

"No. Just away."

We threw some snacks and water bottles in a bag and grabbed the baby backpack carrier. We went for a long hike. It was nice, apart from a few close calls trying to find a place to pee on short notice. And excepting the nagging thought in the back of my mind that eventually we would have to come home.

Eventually we did. Greg watched Gabby while he had me take a long bath. I got Gabby to sleep. While he took a quick shower. Greg gave me a back rub.

"If things are still rough on Monday, I want you to go to the doctor, okay?"

"Yeah," I meant it. Maybe I was crazy. I was fully

prepared to accept that possibility. "Thanks for today. It really was good to get out of the house." I dreaded what sleep might bring, but I felt more whole, more myself than I had in a while. Part of me wondered how much of the disposal's influence was just my own head. If it wasn't real I was pretty sick, but being sick felt like something that maybe I could face if Greg was there to help me through it.

He held my hand until I fell asleep. And that's the last thing I remember.

"Until Greg found you?" the doctor asks.

"Yeah."

"So you remember that part?"

"Mostly. I think."

"What do you remember?"

"Screams mostly. Pain."

"Whose?"

"Mine, Greg's, Gabby's. Probably all three."

"Greg said you were screaming that the disposal wanted the baby but you were giving it yourself instead."

"That's right."

"So do you remember putting your arm into the garbage disposal?"

"No, not really. I just kind of became aware that I was there. And it hurt and there was a lot of screaming."

"But you knew why you were there."

"Yes."

She stares at the heavily wrapped stump that used to be my elbow. "Do you think that you would possibly harm yourself like this again?"

"I—" I try to choose my words. My thoughts are spinning around me too fast. "I hope not."

"Do you feel like you are a danger to yourself or others right now?"

"I honestly don't know."

"We are going to keep you under observation for a while."

"That's probably for the best. Where's Gabrielle?"

The doctor pales. She doesn't meet my eyes. "Once you were out of surgery, Greg took her home to get some rest and get a few things for her. He said he would be back in the morning, but— Well, we'll talk some more tomorrow. "

"You say that like something's wrong. Can I call him? What's going on?"

"Greg's not available to talk on the phone tonight. You've been through quite a bit. We should meet again tomorrow."

The sun is shining through the window. It's still early. I look around for a clock and find it. 5:28, afternoon. "Where are they? Why can't I call Greg?"

"We should talk about it in the morning."

"It's only afternoon now. What's wrong? Where are they? Where's my baby?"

"I'm sorry to have to tell you this, but Greg won't be able to talk to you because he's been arrested."

"What? Why?"

"Apparently, he called the police and turned himself in for— for putting your daughter through the garbage disposal in the kitchen.

My limbs fight the white velcro straps restraining me to the bed frame. The doctor checks that they aren't going anywhere before giving a sad shake of the head to the nurse in the corner as she walks out of the room.

Jinx

"Guards!"

"To the queen!" The response echoed from the hall. Ereldred entered first, sword drawn. The sounds of more armored bodies converging from more distant posts in the palace followed.

"Another threat, your majesty?" Ereldred asked.

"It would seem so." The queen held out a simulacrum of a rat.

Ereldred's chest thundered at him. "You oughtn't touch them until they've been examined, your Majesty."

"Am I a child to be so addressed?" Her eyebrow raised upward slightly.

Ereldred was an idiot. He knew better than to give commands to the queen. But it had been his panic talking. If someone could enter her antechamber to insult her by calling her a rat, they could just as easily enter it to kill her. What if he had arrived too late? He shut that thought behind a cell and locked it. He had a job to do.

A drop of relief spread through his veins when her lips twitch upward slightly at the corners. It was the subtlest of smiles, but Ereldred found his breath stolen by its beauty. He had erred, no doubt, but she was not angry with him. "I apologize for my boldness. What I meant to say, your majesty, is that enemies of the kingdom are afoot. Objects left for you to find could contain a poisoned needle or other dangers planted by the enemies of Hobleduk. I only act out of concern for your wellbeing."

"Your loyalty has never been in question, Captain." Her eyes bored directly into his. She held the stuffed rat out to him. He must have imagined the brush of her fingers as she deposited it into the hand he hadn't realized he'd extended in response. Enough. He was going to die of an aneurysm if he kept this up.

"I... I took the post outside your antechamber myself. No one has approached since you yourself entered. I must respectfully ask your permission to search your chambers for any unauthorized points of entry. It is possible that an interloper could yet be hiding in our very presence."

"You may do what you believe is necessary, Captain Ereldred." The room had become suddenly quiet. Ereldred nearly startled with the realization that this was because the guards were fully assembled and awaiting his orders. He and his monarch were not alone. And he must accept that they never would be. He turned to face the assembly.

"The queen's chambers are compromised by those who would sully her name. Search for any signs of unauthorized entry or evidence of an interloper. Koggins."

"Yes, sir," Koggins said, stepping forward.

"Alert, Alric. Have him take two units and conduct a search of the castle and the grounds. And send me a scully."

"Pardon, but why the scully, sir?"

"The queen may yet be in danger. Not a morsel of food nor a drop of drink must touch the queen's lips without being tasted first, do you understand me?" Ereldred did not often brook with subordinates questioning orders, but it was not every day the captain of the guard requested a scullery maid to attend the queen.

The cabinet door under the sink closed behind Jinx's tail. Mommy was warming up some food in the microwave.

"Where have you been, Jinxy?" Mommy asked.

Jinx wrapped herself between Mommy's legs. Perhaps

Mommy would give her some warm food. Jinx purred. The microwave beeped. Mommy gave her a pinch of something soft and warm to eat off of the kitchen floor before sitting at the table. It was good. Jinx sat at the table too.

"No, Jinx. Mommy's food," Mommy said, holding her arms around the plate. Jinx just wanted to smell it. Maybe lick it a couple of times.

"Where's your mouse, Jinxy?"

Mommy wasn't the smartest. The things she called mice weren't really mice at all. But Jinx humored her sometimes, when she was bored, or when she was in the mood to play, which was never. Or almost never. Well, sometimes. Anyway, silly Mommy didn't seem to know the difference.

Mommy set Jinx on the floor. Jinx hopped back onto the table. Mommy ate quickly and stood up, leaving her plate for Jinx, who began cleaning it off for her. Mommy came back.

"Ugh, Jinx. I can't leave you for two seconds." Jinx knew it made Mommy sad to leave her. Jinx was obviously delightful company.

"I got you a new mouse. One of these days I'll find out what you've done with the other several hundred I've bought you." Jinx watched Mommy toss the "mouse" then looked back at Mommy and yawned. "Or maybe not."

Mommy was sleeping. Jinx watched her for a while. Jinx zoomed through the house a few times. It was best on the carpet where she could really sink her claws in and get some traction. The last lap ended in reverse of how the first had started, with a flying leap onto the foot of Mommy's bed. Mommy was still asleep. Jinx checked all the doors. They were still closed. She checked her food bowl; still empty. Checked the litter, still smelled as it should. Hmm... The "mouse" still laid in the dining room.

Jinx picked it up. It usually took some trial and error, but Jinx was getting faster at opening the cabinet. Still, the slam and rattle each time she didn't pull it quite far enough was satisfying in itself. It was especially fun when Mommy was trying to watch TV. She would keep getting up to try to figure out what Jinx was doing.

Jinx set the "mouse" on the floor of the under-sink cabinet. The Hole was still there. It was just like the one that had a pipe in it. Except there was no pipe. Jinx had been trying for days to figure out where it led. Investigations of the basement yielded no results. But another trial couldn't hurt anything. Jinx stuffed the "mouse" into the hole. It disappeared into the blackness.

The searches had yielded nothing. Captain Ereldred breathed heavily. The queen slept in the next room and he was not sure he could guarantee her safety. He had to be missing something. He ran his hands over the walls, tapped the floorboards, checked the upholstery for tears, anything that might have been missed.

Something soft touched Ereldred's head and landed on the floor next to his feet. He bent down and picked up a stuffed cloth rat. This one was made in garish colors as though it had been sent to mock him. "I might as well fall on my sword," he muttered to himself.

"I would rather find a stuffed rodent than my captain of the guard laying at my feet on the morrow."

"My apologies, your majesty. I will return to my post outside the door if you are awake."

"Why?" Her face was impassive, as always.

"It would not be proper for me to remain without the presence of your lady in waiting."

"She is present." Ereldred's eyes shifted to take in the room that was apparently only occupied by himself until the queen's arrival through her chamber door. "She is presently sleeping."

"So much for having a chaperone through the night." The words were out before Ereldred could stop them.

"Then stay. Keep me company."

"Your majesty, I—"

She closed her eyes and took a deep breath before replying. "I don't want your worship, Captain Ereldred."

He froze.

"I want you to sit down and talk to me. Call me by my first name."

Something in Ereldred's stomach wadded itself up into a painful knot. He couldn't do this. He needed to leave. Now. "I'm sorry. It —"

"Wouldn't be proper. Yes, I know."

Ereldred started to leave. But stopped at her whisper.

"We used to play. As children. Do you remember?"

He was nearly to the door, torn between self preservation and curiosity over where she was going with this line of questioning. "I do."

"The week before my parents died you would have blown on my skinned knee." He remembered it, but if she thought he hadn't worshiped her even then...

"You became queen much too young." He turned toward her. "I'm sorry it happened that way."

She nodded. "Thank you."

A moment of silence passed.

"Good night," He turned to leave once more, "Clarissa."

"It wouldn't be improper, you know," she said quickly.

Ereldred sighed. He wished it were true.

"It would."

"If," she continued, "you were the queen's consort."

"Are you—?"

"I am."

"Why me?"

"Because I see you every day, and I somehow still miss you." Captain Ereldred's eyes definitely did not tear up. He swallowed hard. Surely he would wake to find he'd been dreaming. Perhaps he had gone mad and was in bedlam. He turned again to find that she'd crossed the room already and that he was eye to eye with her. She was taller than he remembered.

Her hands wrapped around his waist. "I'm pretty sure the rats are harmless. I needed to see you alone. I needed to see if you still cared." Her eyes searched him for an answer he was too dazed and speechless to give. She shook him slightly as if to wake him. "Johan, will you marry me?"

His mouth closed over hers needfully breaking a tension he'd carried for years. Growing dizzy, he felt her grip him tighter, holding him upright while she bit at his lip. They stood there for hours. Wrapped in each other's arms. Sometimes talking, sometimes kissing, but mostly in silence. A perfect silence that lacked nothing.

Lady Ermentrude emerged from the queen's chambers shortly after dawn and found them still standing, still embracing, Clarissa's head on Johan's shoulder, a felted green mouse that had fallen unnoticed between their juxtaposed bodies. Meanwhile, Jinx went to bed satisfied that there were no more fake mice in the house to confuse her Mommy.

ENID AND ELVIS

Grandma Enid loved kitsch. Even though she didn't have much money, she made annual pilgrimages to Vegas and Graceland. The junk she collected from souvenir shops covered every surface of her trailer the last time I saw it, fifteen years ago. And it looks no different today. She left me her trailer, for some unfathomable reason. I can sell it for a few thousand if I'm lucky. Most of the contents apart from a few pieces of the more collectible Elvis memorabilia aren't valuable enough to bother trying to sell. In all, her assets will barely cover what I paid for her funeral and the dumpster I'm renting to clean out her place.

It's going to take at least a week evenings of showing up after I leave work at my insurance office just to haul out the literal trash. I came prepared with trash bags, dust masks and dish gloves.

The overwhelming smell of acrid cigarette smoke and old garbage as I step in the flimsy aluminum storm door brings back memories. Not all of them good.

I used to try to clean up her place as a kid sometimes. Before I realized how futile it was. Sometimes if I threw away the wrong bit of trash or moved the wrong collectible she would yell about not respecting her belongings or get huffy and not talk at all.

The worst was when I tried to make a spot in the cabinet for an ugly teapot in the shape of a 70s era Elvis face. It was from when he was drug addled, a bit overweight, and always looked sweaty. It's supposed to be singing but it looks like a weird grimace. I never liked it. Grandma adored it.She made clear to me with her fist that I wasn't allowed to touch it. It only happened once, but I never forgot.

It's still sitting there, next to the avocado green gas stove that's narrower than any reasonable cooking apparatus ought to be. The gaudy thing feels like it's staring at me. I grab a trash bag. It's going to be the first thing to go. But when my fingers brush the cheap porcelain, something stops me. Childhood nostalgia or maybe guilt, knowing it was her favorite thing. Or maybe just an echo of the fear she'd instilled in me of ever touching it again. Either way, it doesn't feel right to get rid of it just yet.

So I start cleaning. It's monotonous work, and I feel like an intruder. I still feel like the Elvis teapot is staring at me somehow. Maybe some music will take my mind off of it. I feel the strangest urge to listen to Elvis music while I clean. I've never cared for it. Probably misplaced sentimentality or sheer boredom, but it wouldn't surprise me if that's all that Grandma Enid had. Even though I was never allowed in Grandma Enid's room as a kid, I know exactly where her cds are, in a little cabinet on her bedside table. I put one in the cd player on the dresser and fire up the music. I head back to my trash bag, but I feel less like cleaning now. I turn up "You Ain't Nothin' but a Hound Dog" and have a seat at the kitchen table, still covered in trash and rodent droppings.

Elvis's stare from the ugly teapot doesn't seem as menacing now. Maybe I'll take it home. I wasn't particularly close to Grandma Enid, but she did babysit me as a kid. I should probably keep some memento of her.

Back in my apartment, Elvis looks disapprovingly at me from the kitchen as I eat my dinner. He seems so out of place here.

I bring the teapot back to Grandma Enid's the next day. He seems happier here. I turn on the music first thing when I come in. I need a cigarette. I've never smoked a day in my life, but there's a first time for everything. I know the Winstons are in the drawer above the cabinet with the Cds without having to look for them.

I sit at the table and take a long drag, listening to the King, as Elvis looks on approvingly. Everything is right in the world.

I take Elvis home with me again. My apartment feels so cold and empty. I really ought to get some quilted house dresses and maybe some little figurines to brighten up the walls. Elvis looks lonely. I dismiss the thought that a teapot could miss anybody, especially Grandma Enid. But then again, it might be the only one. That makes me feel sad. That no one misses her. How lonely that must have been.

In my room, I carefully remove the teapot lid and set it on the nightstand. I cradle Elvis under the covers, and I dream of making a pilgrimage to Graceland.

I give notice to my apartment manager the next morning. I don't bother calling in at work. The agency doesn't need me. Or was it a convenience store? I'm fuzzy on the details. I need to retire anyway, no, I'm twenty seven. Or is it seventy two?

I breathe in the scent of cigarettes at the door of the trailer and gently place the teapot back on the counter. Elvis is home and so am I. I make my way to the closet and grab my favorite house dress. The phone rings and I pick up.

"Hello? Yes, this is Enid speaking. What do you want?"

-4-

BED

ROOMS

A Place to Rest Your Head

Elsie Munroe

There are few, if any, places in the world that can rival the respite one finds in their own bedroom. The bedroom is also a controlled space. If the door to a bedroom is closed when guests arrive, they are unlikely to wander in by mistake. All this to say, that a bedroom should reflect your comforts and personality more so than any other room in the home. It will seldom be judged by anyone but yourself.

In the confines of one's own bedroom, one is more free to be herself than anywhere else. So let loose! Want pink walls? Enjoy! Want a plain bedspread rather than floral chenille? No one but your husband will know. And if he complains, you can always decorate the walls with his entrails. Just think how soundly you'll sleep knowing your space is to your liking!

Many women prefer to keep their room spartan for ease of cleaning. There is nothing wrong with this approach. And indeed there are many advantages.

In general, it is wise to adhere to the following

guidelines. 1. Wash sheets weekly and dry on the line for a fresh, sun-kissed scent. 2. Put your laundry away as soon as you bring it in to avoid both clutter and wrinkles. 3. For a bright and airy look, hydrogen peroxide from the druggist works wonders on removing persistent blood stains. 4. For particularly spirited dismembering, you may wish to lay out a painter's drop cloth or tarpaulin on anything you do not wish to scrub.

As always, try a few systems out, see what you can manage well, and choose what works best for you and your home.

Happy homemaking!

GUM

The wad of gum Josie had been chewing seemed bigger in Josie's mouth than it had when she started chewing it to stay awake to finish her essay. It felt as though it were on the verge of melting, with bits of it sticking to her dental work. She had just finished her assignment, six pages of a research paper for AP English, and was beyond ready to fall onto the bed next to her desk, toothbrush be damned. She needed to get rid of the gum though. She pulled out the little trash can from under the desk, and tried to spit the uncomfortable wad into the Target bag that her mom used to line it.

The gum was too melty and stringy. Josie felt slightly like gagging as she had to reach into her mouth and pull the wad out with her fingers. Little bits of it still clung to her teeth and in the recesses between her cheeks and gums. Gross.

She made her way to the bathroom and brushed her teeth, but despite brushing for at least two full minutes, an astoundingly long time given how wiped she was from hours on end of procrastination driven essay writing, her teeth felt like they were coated in something plastic-y or rubbery. She chalked it up to being sleep deprived and collapsed into bed.

Midi steel drums blaring a jarringly upbeat time from Josie's cell woke her up as usual. She got up and spit out her gum. Huh. Hadn't she done that before she'd gone to bed? Apparently not. Perhaps she had dreamed it. But her teeth felt wrong. Slick and sticky. She opted to skip breakfast due to the odd sensation and brushed her teeth twice instead. Three times. Hard. It would have to do.

"Josie, gum isn't allowed in class," her first period teacher told her. She didn't realize when she'd begun chewing it. It had no particular flavor, it was just there. She must have absentmindedly gotten it out on the bus without realizing it.

Three subsequent teachers said the same. By the time lunch came around Josie was sure that she had spit out the same wad of gum at least four times. She spat it out once more before joining the lunch line. She punched in her code to buy her rectangular piece of pizza, ice cream scoop serving of canned corn, and a chocolate milk roughly the size of a thimble and found a seat at her usual table. Her stomach rumbled. Between her late night typing session and skipping breakfast, her body was begging for whatever calories she could get. She spat some gum into a napkin and took a bite of pizza. Breadcrumbs and cheese floated in a sea of slick rubbery goo. Bile threatened to replace the pizza. She spat the dubious mixture of pizza and gum into her napkin and pushed her tray away.

89

Nichole asked her for a piece of gum and didn't believe her when Josie said she didn't have any. "Seriously? You've been chewing gum all day," Nichole had said. Josie didn't want to sound crazy, so she didn't say anything.

Josie got a text that afternoon that her dad would be working late again. No surprise. She tried to keep up with homework and her usual routines in between spitting out gum and not eating anything all day.

Josie's toothbrush hardly felt like it touched her teeth. She woke up several times throughout the night to spit out wads of gum. She woke up with gum in her hair and painstakingly removed it with the help of a google search and some ice.

Josie didn't want to sound crazy, so she didn't say anything. Teachers and friends began to notice the bags under Josie's eyes and the gaunt look to her face, but they didn't want to seem rude so they said nothing.

The worst part was at night. Josie could hardly sleep for removing string gobs of gum from her mouth at least once an hour. Josie was missing assignments, zoning out during instruction, fighting microbursts of sleep at her desk or even while walking between classes.

Josie had given up trying to get gum out of her hair. Her father's hair clippers had been just the thing for giving herself a gum-free buzz cut. Josie's stomach never stopped aching, but she could only manage water and a seemingly never-ending supply of gum.

Josie didn't want to sound crazy, so she didn't say anything. Teachers and friends began to wonder if Josie was on drugs or if she had developed an eating disorder, but they didn't want to presume so they said nothing.

That is, until the day that Josie didn't come to school. Then the whispers began. Josie had always been the kid with perfect attendance. Even if she was sick, her father didn't have anyone to stay home with her in elementary school, so she'd just gotten in the habit of just showing up no matter what. She figured being miserably sick at school was no worse than being miserably sick at home.

Her father found her in her bed the next morning. The third day that Josie was missing from school, the counselor, Mrs. Jacobs, came in to gently inform all of Josie's classmates that Jessie had died in her sleep. It seemed that she had choked on some gum.

Dust

It is estimated that approximately twenty to fifty percent of household dust is composed of dead skin cells. Jordan had not dusted in a very long time. First, her life had been too hectic. Her husband, Greg, had not been an easy person to live with. But a lot of that had been her fault.

Greg worked longer hours than Jordan. It made sense that he would be upset if dinner wasn't ready and there were dishes piled in the sink. It would be selfish of her to put her feet up after a four hour shift behind a cash register. Greg worked hard. Sometimes ten hour days or more and his job paid the bills. Not hers.

She had to pull her weight in other ways. She was responsible for the housework, the groceries, and such. It was her job to make sure that Greg was taken care of and to help him manage his stress.

Greg had a ton of work stress and it needed an outlet. It wasn't like he beat her or anything, but sometimes he just dishwasher, the space looked as though something approaching a capable adult lived there.

The dryer beeped a reminder. Jordan filled her arms with hot, fluffy, sweet-smelling bedding and wanted to do this again every day of her life. Then she remembered the dust people. Were they people? Had they been a figment of her imagination?

Jordan tip-toed up the stairs and peeked under the bed. A flurry of movement stopped. Again the dust motes turned toward her, but this time the silence didn't last. The whispers broke out again, but they were different. In unison. Melodic. They were... singing?

Jordan stood and tried to make sense of what she'd seen. What she'd felt. There was a connection between herself and this dust.

She made the bed and it never looked more warm or inviting than at that moment. She climbed in and fell asleep quickly to the soft murmur of voices beneath her, knowing that she would wake up and begin again tomorrow.

Jordan woke the next morning to the murmur of the dust people. She checked under the bed before she began her day. Bits of carpet fuzz had been moved around in an arrangement that Jordan knew was supposed to resemble her own face surrounded by some sort of symbols. The scale of such a work to beings so small must be gargantuan. Jordan's heart warmed to the dust people again.

She wanted to protect them. How easy it would be for someone to come along and vacuum up their entire civilization. Was it a civilization? Jordan wondered. No, of course not. It was dust. But dust that built structures and sang songs and developed symbols? Maybe civilization was the correct term.

A thought occurred to Jordan. She could not protect them if she defaulted on the mortgage and the house were repossessed. Jordan knew roughly where the Important Papers and things were kept, but she'd never done anything with them herself.

She dug through the file cabinet in the desk until she found all of the websites, all of the passwords she needed. The mortgage, she found, was set up on autopay. So at least that was taken care of. She needed to check balances to see it there was enough to cover it. For the moment, there was, but she probably wouldn't make it another month without income. The store. She would apply at the store. She also found a file with insurance information and contacted the company to find that she was to receive roughly one hundred thousand dollars on Greg's life insurance policy.

The house was safe. The dust people wouldn't be hoovered by a realtor anytime soon. Jordan spent the rest of the day filling out job applications, taking breaks to feed herself real food, even if it did come from boxes and bags.

has a picket fence with room for a dog and white shutters on the windows. I keep the shutters and the drapes to the bedroom windows closed, as Mr. Munroe's medical condition makes him sensitive to light. He has been unable to work outside the home for some years now, but he's holding up remarkably well. You could say it's due to my efforts, but I believe it is my love's tenacity that is responsible rather than any efforts on my part.

All I contribute is a few stitches here, some stuffing there. I get spare parts on occasion when I'm out of town. I do pride myself on being very choosy. After all, Mr. Monroe is the best of all men.

Strange Rooms

to another, losing sight of the task you started with. Return to your zone and continue in order to make progress.

3. Is there enough space for this item? If the answer is no, consider if there are other things you can do without. Is there another thing that can also do this job? Is this something that is truly worth the space it is taking up? If so, do you really need more shelving? It can be tempting to think you do not have enough storage, when in reality, what you need are fewer belongings taking up space in you home and your mind.

When you have thoroughly edited your inventory, every item should have a logical and easily accessible home. But you likely have a pile of "stuff" that you now need to get out of your home. It is important to choose the best option for your situation. Some communities have a center that accepts charitable donations. Some of the larger or more valuable items, might be worth the trouble of selling. But unfortunately, you will often find that items you don't need, no one else wants either. In this case, it may be worthwhile to pay the expense for a special pickup with your garbage service. If for some reason you are unable to afford this, or if you have items that they do not collect, I find that the easiest solution is to deposit the items in the home of a newly deceased person.

And how does one find the home of a newly deceased person, you may ask? The possibilities are endless!

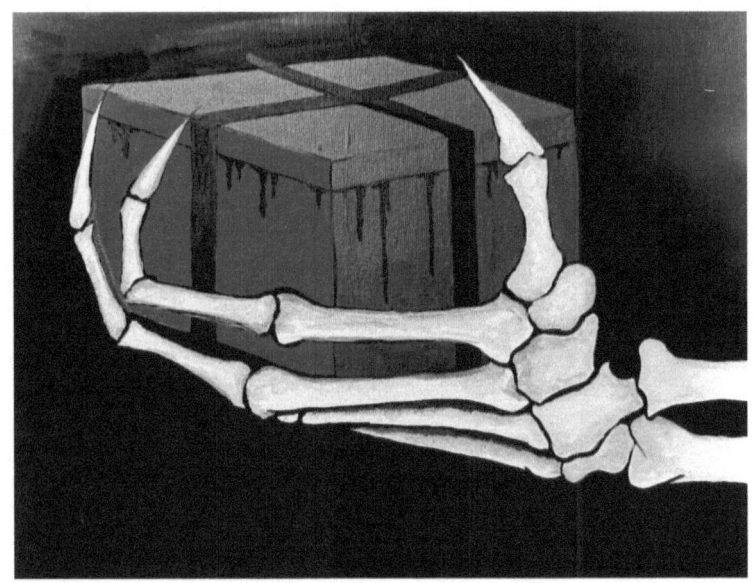

"A gift for you."

A Christmas Gift for Adelaide

Originally published in
TWISTED TALES OF HOLIDAY HORROR by
The Sisterhood of the Black Pen

"Don't you have any friends you would like to invite to the Christmas party this year?"

She didn't. Adelaide was occasionally invited to tag along with someone or other, but she rather suspected that people just felt sorry for her. She didn't want their pity or their friendship.

"No, Mama."

"Really, dear, you must make some effort. Oh, your grandmother sent a note that she'll be joining us for dinner this evening. I would like you to help Cook downstairs."

"Of course, Mama." Glad for any excuse to stop

embroidering pointless flowers, Adelaide set her needlework on the window seat and started across the room.

"ADELAIDE!" Adelaide stopped. "Ladies do not thunder about their homes like elephants. If that is how you comport yourself at school, I have half a mind to withdraw you before the next term begins. It is not uncommon for girls to marry at your age, Adelaide. You are a woman. And you must conduct yourself in a manner befitting one who can run her household with grace."

"Yes, Mama." Adelaide rolled her eyes as she straightened and used the sweeping walk that she had so often practiced with a book upon her head. She felt like a marionette, and her mother the puppeteer. "And don't forget to put on your apron, dear. We can't have you spoiling your dresses."

"Yes, Mama." Adelaide answered over her shoulder through gritted teeth. She walked in her more graceful, womanly stride until she was safely downstairs before she resumed "thundering about." In fact she stomped about a few times just because no one was looking. At least Nona was coming. Nona and her parents didn't always get on. Adelaide liked her better for it.

A wave of heat hit Adelaide as she entered the kitchen. Cook had been working all week preparing for their family Christmas dinner. The larder was full of beautiful cookies and cakes which she had been explicitly instructed not to touch until the party. Adelaide wasn't sure why everyone thought it so very likely that she would sneak down to devour several dozen cookies and cakes. Perhaps they just relished the opportunity to set more limits on her.

Cook was at work peeling potatoes. A round, red-faced woman, Cook was the only servant in the employ of their household. She served as chef, laundress, nursemaid and did most of the real work of the household, though Adelaide's mother wasn't above allowing her to assist when Cook was likely to be busy. Cook wasn't exactly pleasant to be around, but she was the only person who let Adelaide get her hands dirty, which she found that she enjoyed. Adelaide especially loved when she got to punch down a bowl of risen dough and watch it deflate around the indentation left by her fist.

Adelaide also appreciated that Cook also didn't gossip. She never said anything about the day when she walked in on Adelaide punching bread dough as though it were her mortal enemy until her arms hurt and she didn't feel angry anymore. She rolled up her sleeves and put on a serviceable apron from the hook on the wall.

"Mother sent me to help you with dinner. What shall I do?" Adelaide asked.

"Oh, bless her," Cook said. "The roast is nearly done, thank heavens, so I'll just need you to take care of the sprouts. When you've done that, you can cut the lard and butter into the flour for the biscuits. I set it in a crock outside last night to make sure it's good and cold, so mind you don't overwork it.

After that, it's just finishing touches, so you can get cleaned up and set the places."

Adelaide did as she was told. The sprouts didn't involve much more than cutting them off the woody green stalk. Cook took over from there. Adelaide cut the butter and lard cut into the flour mixture until the texture resembled something between damp sand and fine pebbles, then pressed it into a ball that magically held together by her hands warming the fat just enough. There was satisfaction in it, but not as much as pounding bread dough.

Shortly after she finished setting the last place, the bell at the door rang. Adelaide rushed to hang up her kitchen apron before she answered, barreling into the foyer at a near run. Rather than receiving guests, Adelaide received instead a cold glare from her mother who had apparently reached the foyer first.

"Welcome! Do come in out of the cold," Mother said looking with some confusion over Nona's shoulder. "Did you not employ a carriage? You know we would have sent ours for you if you had only asked."

"Nonsense. A brisk walk in the winter air is good for the constitution."

"I only worry that you'll catch your death of cold, especially at your age."

"I'm still your mother, Wilhelmina. And I'll thank you to leave an old woman to do as she pleases."

Mama sighed and ushered Nona into the parlor. Adelaide trailed behind wishing she'd had at least a moment before her mother had spoiled Nona's visit.

"What a lovely Christmas tree you have this year," Nona said, taking in the berry garlands and candles adorning the tree.

"Yes, our Adelaide did much of the decorating herself. We can light the candles for you if you would like."

"Don't worry about that," said Nona. "I will be back for the party. I wouldn't miss giving our Adelaide her Christmas gift for the whole world."

Adelaide grinned. Nona always gave her the same thing. A doll. Adelaide, of course, had not played with any of her dolls in a very long time. She was sixteen, after all. But she looked forward to receiving them just the same. They weren't like the rag dolls that many children in the town had, or even like the fancier dolls you could buy at the new-fangled department stores in the city. The dolls she received from Nona were works of art. Adelaide even had a special case in her room constructed for their display.

Nona ordered the most delicate china for their faces, hands and feet. The bodies were rag cloth stuffed with sawdust, but the china was so intricately formed that Nona must sacrifice dearly to afford them. The faces were exquisitely hand-painted, and they were always dressed in a festive Christmas gown. But their crowning glory was their beautiful hair. Locks so soft and vibrant and fashionably styled, Nona's dolls were the envy of every girl who had seen them, and many who had merely heard about them too.

"Dinner will be served presently. Won't you have a seat?"

The three of them had just sat down when Adelaide's father entered.

"Good evening, Mrs. Winthrop," he bowed his head as he addressed Nona dryly. Nona flashed a glare at him.

"Forgive my habit, Nona. It is unusual for a married woman to insist upon being called by her first name."

" Mr. Winthrop didn't die yesterday."

"Of course, may he rest in peace."

"Henry, mother just walked all this way to join us." Wilhelmina said with condescension thinly disguised as admiration.

"What's that? But you'll catch your death of cold, my dear Mrs. Winthrop. A woman of your age ought to take more care."

"If I die, while walking in the outdoors, I will die content."

Adelaide did her best to hide a snort. Nona always said the very things that Adelaide wished she could.

"I know your feelings on this subject, Mrs. Winthrop, but it really is unheard of that you should choose to live alone and uncared for in the winter of your life." Adelaide sat silent and alert, knowing a conversation on this topic would seldom end amicably. "As an upstanding member of this community, I am often questioned how I can allow you to continue thus."

"Yes, Mother," joined Wilhelmina. "You know we have ample space for you here."

"You know my answer." Nona looked still and calm in much the same way as a bear trap before it springs.

"But why, Mother? Why don't you have one of the guest rooms? Cook does most of the household work, and you would not have to toil so in keeping your own home."

"And what would I do with myself then?" Nona laughed. "Serve as a decorative lamp? A bookend perhaps?" Nona said with a smirk. "No, dear, Henry has done well in life, but such a life is not for me."

"I really must insist, Mrs. Winthrop. For your own welfare, I cannot allow -"

"You listen well, Henry." The sudden harshness of her voice filled the room with a chill. Everyone froze. All traces of Nona's characteristic smirk were gone. It seemed like ages before she continued. "For forty years, my husband made decisions for my welfare. And for seventeen years before that, my parents did the same. When George departed, I made a promise. Never again. Never. If age is good for nothing else, let me tell you that I have experience enough to know my own mind." A long silence strained against the passage of time.

"Mother, I'm sorry if we offended you. But if you would only permit us to hire some help for you, we needn't worry so. I'm sure Cook would know someone." Nona gave an exasperated sigh. Conversations like this had become more and more frequent in the last few years. It was a bit odd that Nona would choose to live alone with family so close by and more than able to provide for her, but Nona always valued her independence, at least as long as Adelaide had known her.

"No thank you, dear. I have no use for help of any kind." Nona's smirk returned. Her voice had returned to its usual tone, one of calm irony. "Servants talk. A woman must have some secrets. I can't bear to think what might be said of the rats in my cellar in kitchens across the county. What scandal!" Nona's eyes twinkled. Adelaide supposed that Nona was ribbing her father.

Nona's cellar did have rats, though. She kept the basement locked on account of them. Adelaide once stayed the night at Nona's little house past the edge of the town. She hardly slept for the scratching and banging that the rats made in the cellar. When asked why she didn't merely trap them or lay out poison, she always said that she didn't really want to hurt them, just discourage them from traipsing about her kitchen. "George would never have allowed rats in the cellar," she would say with a smile. "But they don't harm anything so long as they are confined."

Dinner passed pleasantly and uneventfully compared to the conversation in the parlor. Nona even permitted her father to have her driven back to her home rather than walk in the dark and the cold.

Adelaide couldn't sleep. Tomorrow was Christmas Eve. She no longer received toys, with the exception of Nona's dolls, which hardly qualified. But Adelaide still had the sense that things felt more magical and exciting at Christmas. She grabbed a match from the drawer of her bedside table and relit her lamp. She then lifted her mattress to retrieve the book she'd hidden there.

She had found it coming home from school one day, or rather, she narrowly missed being hit in the head as it flew out of a window. Its previous owners seemed to be having an argument about it, stoking Adelaide's curiosity as to why anyone would dislike a book so much as to actually throw it away. The tattered cover was nondescript, reading, "Fanny by Anonymous." She had never heard of Fanny, nor did she know who Anonymous was, but once she began reading, she very much doubted her mother would approve of either of them.

Adelaide wasn't completely ignorant about her body, as some girls were. Her mother had allowed her to learn about her menstrual cycle. She never discussed it of course, merely marked the pages in a copy of a book called Maidenhood, Marriage and Maternity, instructing Adelaide to read only those. Adelaide read the whole thing. If she was to be relegated to a future of ladies societies and screaming babies, she thought it fair that she should at least have a rudimentary understanding of the private duties of being a wife and mother

118

as well as those openly discussed. Unfortunately the text was more poetic than practical regarding such things.

Fanny and her unknown creator, however, proved to be a much more exhaustive source. Fanny's exploits of men (and women), both married and unmarried, were something else entirely. They had nothing to do with duty to one's husband or the creation of souls. Fanny lived for pleasure without constraint. She knew what she wanted and took only that, nothing more or less.

While Adelaide did not at all look forward to physical intimacy of any kind or with persons of any description, she wanted... Something that Fanny had. Something that Nona seemed to have as well. Fanny and Nona were both free in a way that Adelaide admired but feared that she would never be able to claim. That was why Adelaide kept Fanny hidden under her mattress. Fanny made her feel strong.

The next morning, after being fussed about to make sure that her Christmas gown was perfect and that she was perfect and that she would mind her manners, and not stand so close to the fire so as to catch her skirts on fire, and whom she must dance with, and with whom she must speak before the evening's end, Adelaide decided to call on Nona. She did not mention to anyone where she was going. She just made her vague excuses as people do when they need to relieve themselves, and grabbed her winter things and disappeared. She had to get out, somehow. She would be that free, at least. It wasn't just the party that weighed on her, but all of the expectations to follow. A life devoid of joy. She had to get out somehow.

The air on the eve of the holiday was bitingly cold, but the sun was bright, lending a false expectation of warmth. Adelaide had planned accordingly, though, and the brisk walk soon had her feeling toasty with her woolens underneath and her hat, scarf, and hand muff supplementing the warmth of her cape.

She arrived on Nona's step with bright red patches on her cheeks and nose from the juxtaposition of her own warmth with the exposure of her face. She knocked three times and waited. No answer came. Perhaps Nona hadn't heard the first time. She knocked louder. She heard footsteps approaching slowly. The door opened and Adelaide took in her grandmother's face. She looked pale and pained.

"Oh, Adelaide, I am so glad that it's you, dear."

"Are you quite well, Grandmother?"

"Nothing the sight of you and some afternoon tea can't fix," she replied. "Come in, come in!" Nona's usually papery skin was clammy, her breathing strained.

"Shall I run for the doctor?" It was a long shot, but she would try to catch a motor carriage, if she could. The things were terribly noisy, but it would get her to the doctor quickly if one chanced to pass by.

"Heavens, no. I have a number of things to attend to

today. It is fortunate you happened along though, as I could use your help."

"Yes, of course." Adelaide walked her grandmother, who had never before needed such help, to her chair, then hurried to put the kettle on. "What was it you wished to attend to today?" Adelaide asked. Nona looked as though she were getting weaker by the moment.

"I will need you to make my excuses for the party."

"Of course." Adelaide said. "Are you sure I shouldn't run for the doctor?"

"Under no circumstance will you bring the doctor or anyone else here today." Nona's eyes flared as she spoke with a firmness that belied her physical state. She sighed and closed her eyes for a long moment. "I'm going to take some beauty rest presently. There's a letter from my solicitor in the drawer of the writing desk, a Mr. Dawkins. I would like you to read it while I sleep. But before that, I want to see you open your Christmas gift. It is sitting on the hall table."

Adelaide retrieved the oblong box from the hall. It was wrapped in brown paper with a beautiful red ribbon. She sat before Nona and opened it. Adelaide couldn't imagine anything more beautiful than the doll that lay inside. The clothing was finer than any ball gown she had ever seen. Green silk. The face was molded and painted not as a child, but as a woman. And the hair put the dress to shame. Red ringlets. So distinctive.

Adelaide had only known one person to have hair that

fiery. Herald, the butcher's son with a cleft lip. Of course, he had always worn his hair short, which was a shame really. She had almost forgotten about him since he had set off to become a sailor or some such about a year ago.

"She's beautiful," Adelaide said when she had recovered her ability to speak. "Thank you, Grandmother."

"Thank you." Nona smiled weakly. "Making your dolls was the greatest joy I've ever known. Did you know that George died the very day you were born?"

Adelaide nodded. "I've seen his stone at the graveyard."

"I was so glad that you never met him. I knew that you would be stronger for it." Nona's voice was growing weaker and she worked hard to swallow. Why had Nona not asked for a doctor? Though now she feared it might be too late if she did go. But perhaps it wasn't too late even now. "When the life drained from his eyes, not two hours before your mother was bearing down, I felt in my bones that you wouldn't bow down and let your life be dictated to you. I've always loved you for it. I've lived every day since, endeavoring to be a worthy example. I knew you would have no other."

The tears that stung Adelaide's eyes made a trail down each cheek. This was goodbye. "I love you too. Grandma, please don't go." Adelaide's throat was so tight, her voice came out somewhere between a squeak and a whisper.

"I'm tired now," Nona whispered. "Read the letter and let an old woman rest."

Adelaide nodded and walked to the writing desk, listening to Nona's shallow, labored breaths. She found an envelope just where Nona had said it would be and opened it. It was dated months ago.

Mrs. Winthrop,

Upon receipt of the signed copy of your will, I have returned your handwritten original as requested.

Best wishes,

James Dawkins,

Solicitor

THE LAST WILL AND TESTAMENT OF NONA WINTHROP

I, Nona Winthrop of Carrollton Village, Westvalia, declare this to be my last will and testament.

I am of sound mind, in spite of the fact that I am seventy three and female. And furthermore,I would like to point out that these things have very little to do with each other contrary to what some may believe. This will was written without undue influence or duress, since my husband has been dead for over sixteen blessed years. At the time of this will, I am happily widowed and mother to Wilhelmina

123

Babbage, formerly Wilhelmina Winthrop. She has chosen her life and has no need of my worldly effects. And as she and her doting husband are so busy as to hire out their housework I shall not burden them with executorship, and leave that task jointly to Mr. Dawkins and my granddaughter, Adelaide. Since I have no debts and I already have arrangements with the undertaker, Dawkins made sure of that before he agreed, this is really just a formality.

I leave everything, from the spiders in the attic to the rats in the cellar to Adelaide, to do with as she will. My only other request is that Adelaide should be the only person to enter my home until she has formally taken possession and thereby has the right to invite only whom she chooses.

I wish to include here a few last comments to my dear Adelaide. Always choose your path. Don't forget to feed the rats. And never forget, a woman must have her secrets.

Additional pages followed with signatures and notarizations and legal things that Adelaide didn't care to read. Adelaide froze. The sound of Nona's breathing had stopped. Adelaide held her hand in front of her grandmother's mouth and nose. When she felt nothing, she checked for a heartbeat, and again, found nothing. Nona was gone. Adelaide's tears consumed her. Nona was the only person who had ever seemed to understand her, the only one whom she had ever really loved. After a time, Adelaide ran out of tears. She read Nona's words to her again. Always choose your path. Don't forget to feed the rats. And never forget, a woman must have her secrets.

Nona would never completely be gone. Adelaide knew that nothing could ever undo the spark that Nona had lit in her spirit. She would be free. She would find that something, that passion for life, she wouldn't settle for less. No more would she take orders day after day, no more would she anxiously anticipate a tedious, loveless marriage with someone who would treat her like a child. Because Nona had walked that path for her, learned those lessons for her. Nona had shown her the way. Adelaide would be forever grateful. She only wished she could tell Nona how grateful she was.

Don't forget to feed the rats. The thought came unbidden to her mind as though it wanted to be known. Like it had some significance beyond its face value. It was an odd request, to be sure. But one she could honor. Rats weren't so bad, after all. She filled a bowl with water and grabbed a slice of bread off the table and turned her eyes to the keys that hung on hooks by the door. One of them must fit. She really hoped she wouldn't have to rummage in Nona's skirt pockets to find it. Thankfully the first key she tried proved to be the correct one.

Adelaide opened the door and a surprisingly sharp odor met her nose as she began her descent into the dark cellar.

Something moved. She jumped and nearly screamed as she tripped backward toward the step she had just left. The thing was ghostly white and making a haunting moaning noise. No, crying. A low despairing cry that was not meant for an audience but could not be helped. It was a person. Or it had been. It was male, a fact which she largely knew thanks to Fanny, but this thing hardly looked human at all. Its naked flesh was so very white and pulpy, like a large piece of fat from the butcher's shop. It was writhing on the floor like a worm, tied at the feet and hands. Sores interrupting the white flesh oozed a foul liquid. It had apparently been here for some time, pallid and atrophied from unknown days in the dark and damp. A bundle of rags obscured its mouth and muffled its cries.

Adelaide ran back up the stairs and slammed the door, her breathing much harder than the few steps she had taken warranted as she tried to sort out her feelings. "A woman must have her secrets," Nona had said. No wonder she didn't want people poking about her house. But she must have wanted Adelaide to know. Nona had specifically said to feed the rats. She must have known that Adelaide would come upon the wretch. Why?

It suddenly dawned on her, that white, fleshy thing was "the rats" that had scratched in the night and at their tea parties. Adelaide's thoughts raced. She should tell someone, surely. But that would leave Nona's reputation in disgrace, as well as her family by association. And there was something else too. Something in the back of her mind that she wasn't sure if she was ready to unbox just yet. She couldn't ignore that box in the back of her mind forever. It begged to be opened.

When she regained control over her breathing, she took up the bread and water again and opened the cellar door once more. Since she knew what to expect, the shock wasn't so great this time.

Looking calmly at the thing on the floor, she couldn't explain to herself why she couldn't think of it as a human. It was a detestable thing that was best hidden. The pale soft thing sitting in its own putrescence looked more like a slug in a slime trail to her than a rat. The part of her from inside the box in the back of her mind wanted to pour salt on it to see if it would shrivel up.

She laid the bread and water on the floor. She didn't want to touch the thing more than she had to, but she had to remove the gag so it could eat. It raised its head toward her and seemed to be pleading, but she couldn't make out the words. The top of its head had been shaved, but some stubble was making its way through. Bright red. She untied and pulled out the bundle of rags and paused in recognition.

That mouth. With its unmistakable cleft lip.

So that's who this thing had once been.

Herald.

It made more unintelligible noises. That was interesting. It had no tongue. Probably for the best. That hair. That beautiful hair she had so admired on her doll. It had probably taken a year or more to grow it out. Such pains. And on her behalf.

Adelaide took in her surroundings rather than watch the filthy thing work its empty mouth. There were mounds of something spaced evenly along the walls. It took a while to adjust her eyes to the dark and work out what they must be. Corpses. Sixteen, if she counted the one still breathing. One for every year. Tears came to Adelaide's eyes. She would open that box at last.

They were so... beautiful.

Not the bodies themselves, of course, but the gift. These were Nona's joy. Laid before her was the freedom that Nona had found. For her. The life that Nona wanted to share with her, beautifully displayed in order of their state of decomposition, though they were more desiccated than rotten except where they met the floor.

They were made with such love, just like her beautiful dolls. Adelaide finally knew what she had been missing. Nona had been showing her the way all along, and she could never ask for a better gift. Adelaide smiled a bittersweet smile as she ascended the staircase. She would have to remember to go back down in a few minutes to replace the gag before she left to take care of Nona's affairs.

After all, a woman must have her secrets.

SUMP PUMP

The child stood at the edge of a hole.

A sump pump, her mother called it.

The child knew better.

It was a hole.

The house around the hole was old,

Over a hundred years.

It was built around the hole.

The hole existed before the house was built.

The hole was dark.

The water in it was darker.

The child could not see the bottom.

The hole knew there wasn't one.

The hole had swallowed women and men.

It had swallowed compsognathus.

The hole had seen the creation of the world around it

And rejected all but formless matter.

It wore the water like a wolf in a sheepskin,

Like a universe in a teaspoon.

The child looked into the hole,

And the hole looked into the child.

TRISTAN AND SABINE
Originally published in
TWISTED TALES OF HALLOWEEN HORROR
by the
Sisterhood of the Black Pen

-TRISTAN-

"You've forgotten the lights again."

"Hmm?" I sigh. I must have actually dozed off without realizing it. I wish to God he hadn't woken me. There are precious few nights I fall asleep restfully. And I know damn well I left them all lit.

"You've left the lamp lit and several candles too. I'm afraid that if every innkeeper on the continent charges us for refilling the lamps every night, it will eat up any savings of sharing a room. We may have to cut our travels short and return to Cambridge with barely a pamphlet's worth of research."

"Oh, sorry, Professor. I assumed you would be along shortly, so I left it as a courtesy."

"I've explained to you before that if you retire early, as you make a habit of doing, that I don't need you to leave the

131

lamps and candles alight. I don't have a complicated routine of an evening, Tristan." He splashes some water from the basin on his face and dries it. "And I should think that the innkeeper would likewise prefer that their establishment to not be burnt to a crisp on my account."

"Of course. Terribly sorry." I make an effort to channel my genuine shame into the appearance of repentance, wracking my brain for how I can contrive to keep the lights on again tomorrow without arousing suspicion.

"I'm well aware of my privilege in being able to afford to travel abroad for my research, but I am not so rich as to not notice the extra charges laid on us for the extra candles and oil."

"Of course." I'm running out of ideas, and I know that the professor is right. It's exceedingly wasteful of me to light the lamps while it's still daylight and to leave them lit while no one truly needs them. "It was terribly forgetful of me. I will try to remember to extinguish them tomorrow."

"You can blow them out now. I'm done washing up."

I blow out the lamp on the table and all but one of the three candles around the room that are burning low as he climbs into the bed across the room. I glance over my shoulder to make sure Sabine isn't looking before I hold my wrist over the flame—just long enough to remind me of the light and make me feel as though a part of it is still with me through the night.

It hurts, but I won't be able to sleep anyway. Because God knows I'm a liar. And I know what liars deserve.

-SABINE-

"Not the box," Tristan whispers. Box? I don't have the foggiest idea what he's going on about, but he's had a funny look to him since we lost sight of the village. He just looked a bit white at first, which I attributed to the cold and damp. But then he just stopped walking and stood perfectly still like a man whose soul had left his body until he whispered those words. He doubles over, breathing so hard that it must surely make him dizzy, but he pants for air as a man who is drowning.

"Slow down, man. You're all right. You're all right." I uselessly reassure him until the spell passes. "Are you sure that you're well now?" My voice feels flat in the stillness of the marsh air around us. The innkeeper told us this morning that no one but the Widow Ciobanu lives in "the Waste," the name by which the locals call this boggy stretch of earth, nor do they have any business here. The innkeeper assured us that she was very knowledgeable on the folklore surrounding werewolves, the subject of my newest collection. Perhaps it is only the knowledge that there is not another soul for miles around us, but I had not accounted for how lonely it would feel here. The atmosphere feels like it's never been disturbed in the history of man, and it seems to take no notice of us even now.

"I shall be," Tristan replies, yet his eyes say otherwise. He's young and strong, but he doesn't look well at all. Perhaps

133

some rowdiness from the inn's common room kept him awake, but this is something more. His jaw and neck muscles are tense, and his skin has a clammy pallor that cannot entirely be accounted for by the ever present fog. Perhaps it is fear of losing our way.

I am not prone to the shivers myself, for I bear my faith as an inviolable shield, if not against physical harm, then against anything that might affect my eternal soul. Though, I am wary that we shouldn't stray off the path through the Waste. It's only just made visible by the many years it's been traversed by the members of a single family. The dense fog hangs about us like a white curtain, rendering any objects or persons completely obscured as if they were behind a wall of plaster. I wouldn't like to think of how long a man might wander in the fog if he were to stray but a little.

"I can still see your unease. Is it the fog that troubles you?" I ask.

The path we walk is an unpleasant, almost marshy thing. Grasses grow to either side of it only just visible through the opaque gloom. The ground squelches with our every step. It soaks through my boots and wool stockings, though the rest of me is scarcely drier. The mud and the mist give the impression that they are one and the same—still, stagnant, and unwholesome. A miasma of decaying things hangs about the place.

"No, sir. Well, yes, in a way."

"Do not fear. We shall stick to the path and trust in God to guide us safely. And to guide me in the use of my revolver if necessary. I'm a terrible shot." I would not be eager to use lethal force on a fellow man, of course, particularly not for the mere loss of goods when the man at the receiving end could lose his eternal soul with his last act being one of a sinful nature. But I hope that the appearance of a gun might be enough to deter a highwayman, and it seemed prudent when venturing into old and wild places, such as this, that I should have some means of protection against wild beasts.

"It is not fear, exactly. I have a particular discomfort of not being able to see. So, yes, the fog discomfits me, but it is of little consequence. The innkeeper informed me that the Waste where the Widow Ciobanu resides is more often shrouded in fog than it is not. It cannot be helped." His jaw is set and his eyes downcast. I haven't seen him look so scared, so small, since the first day I saw him at the university.

I had just entered the library for some research on comparative tellings of various bits of Eastern European folklore for my thesis. A boy sat alone at a study table, reading. He was small and thin, verging on frail, but his eyes sparkled with joy. He read as a man who had entered the gates of heaven. He soaked up the delights of the words on the page before him as though they filled a great need. The world around him had ceased to exist entirely. I watched him for a time, wondering what text could enrapture a young man so completely.

"Might I ask what you are reading?" I asked.

At first, the boy did not react to my approach. He was still adrift in a sea of words.

"Excuse me."

He continued reading.

I tried louder. "Excuse me."

He jumped as though he had been caught at something rather shameful and quickly closed his book, sliding it beneath the larger tome chained to the desk.

"Oh, goodness. You gave me quite a start, Professor... I'm sorry, I don't believe we've been introduced."

"Hastings. Forgive me for startling you. I noticed that you seem to be enjoying your book a great deal. Might I ask what you are reading?"

"Oh, yes. Of course." The boy proceeded to show me the impressive looking tome that he had placed on the much smaller book he had been reading.

"Ah, yes. Summa Theologica, the great work of Thomas Aquinas. What is your favorite part?"

"Um, yes, well, the theological premise on the whole, I should think."

I had to bite my tongue not to laugh out loud and scare the little rabbit away or I would have never found anything out about him. "Ah, yes. The theological bits are rather the whole point. Though, to be honest, I find them as dry as tombs." I couldn't help but smile at the boy who was clearly hiding an earnest love for something with an equally earnest ignorance of theology. "But what is this bit sticking out from beneath?" I simply had to know at this point, even if I had to wrest it away from him.

"It," the boy's lip trembled, "It's nothing."

"Come now." I smiled in what I hoped was a disarming and not at all accusing way. It must have worked too, as he handed me the book. It was barely more than a pamphlet really, with a cover of thick paper rather than bound leather. He cringed as I observed it, as though he were expecting a whipping. It was a collection of children's stories, translated from German. I couldn't contain my laughter. "Is this what you were reading?"

His face glowed with shame. "I don't expect that—"

"Young man," I interjected, "there is no shame in taking joy in children's stories. I collect them myself. Children often don't realize how complex and wonderful they are. In fact, I need an assistant to accompany me on an upcoming sabbatical to conduct some research. I would be honored to have such an enthusiastic reader of children's tales to assist me in my own studies of folklore, especially if you have any skill as a translator. What is your name?"

"Tristan, sir. But aren't you terribly upset with me for my duplicity?"

"Nonsense. I couldn't have a better assistant than one who genuinely loves stories as much as I. What sort of research are you doing here?"

"I'm afraid, I– well, none, sir."

"Reading solely for pleasure then?"

"Yes... No... Well, not solely. You see, some of the men in the commons were discussing a lady of their acquaintance who was much changed in appearance of late. Merriweather Fortescue likened her to a 'cinder maid,' and they all laughed when I asked why. Apparently, it is a childhood tale." He lowered his eyes to the ancient oak desk again.

"One with which you were not familiar, I take it. And you are taking steps to remedy this?"

"Yes, sir."

"There are many reasons why a scholar might reference records of folklore and fairytales. I myself make a study of recording them. But I see no reason why a man should try to hide it. The Cinder Maid is a common enough tale, but there are as many variations on it as there are civilizations in the world. Perhaps you know it by another name."

"No." There was a finality in his voice. Not like someone putting their foot down, but like someone who had only just accepted a deep loss and had been asked to exhume it. He did not speak again for several moments. I didn't pressure him. He looked as though he might begin to sob, but he merely sat in silence until he was able to say with all appearances of decorum, "My nurse was... unkind."

-Tristan-

We reach the home of Widow Ciobanu after midday, though it's hard to be certain with the sun hiding behind the Godforsaken fog. I know I shouldn't think such things. I must render every thought captive unto Christ, but I struggle to see Him in this place. The thought makes me shudder.

The widow does not speak a word of English, having spent all her life in this hovel on the marsh. While the professor employed me as his assistant partly because he loved how I saw folklore with such novelty, in reality, I mostly work as his translator in his travels. The professor has spent most of his studies in Latin rather than modern languages, as my tutor had seen fit to teach me in my youth.

My parents spent much time abroad and left me in the care of my nurse, Katie. I was too sickly a child to attend boarding school with other boys my age, so a tutor was arranged for me when I turned ten, and my parents decided I needed a more learned instructor than Katie. The reason for my sickliness became apparent when my new tutor, Mr. Henshaw, decided as a part of my education to develop my physical abilities as well as my mental faculties. We took a walk on a warm day, and he thought it a prime opportunity for a swimming lesson. I shall never forget the look of horror on his face when I removed my shirt. My chest and back were a mass of bruises, young and red, old and yellowish green, deep violet in the intermediate stage. I knew no different. My tutor saw to it that my nurse was dismissed that very day. He was a kind man and a skilled educator, but much damage had already been done to body, mind, and soul.

Hardly a day passes which does not reveal an undiscovered crack that woman left behind in my shattered self. I'm ashamed of my spell in the marsh today. In the past, I've only known myself to have my episodes in the most utter darkness, but apparently, I can lose myself in fog as well. I hardly know what the professor said to me while I was awash in my own brokenness. On a few such occasions in the past I have gone so far as to...

But that is in the past. I must try to do better.

I start as a figure appears in the mist not five feet in front of me. It can only be the Widow Ciobanu, for the innkeeper explained that her family has been the only people to live in the Waste and that no man who values his horse would dare to take it here. She apparently heard our approach and awaited our arrival.

I introduce myself and the professor and explain his aspiration to complete an exhaustive treatise on the folklore surrounding werewolves, indicating that the innkeeper in town had recommended her in particular as something of an expert on the topic. She smiles with teeth broken and worn and bids us welcome into her home.

The hovel of weathered boards, thatch, and mud is scarcely drier than the waste beyond its walls. But there is a fire. The woman's bed lies in one corner, and a table sits before the hearth. It's stained a dark and hideous shade of red that would be shocking had I not, in recent weeks, become inured to the ubiquity of the beetroot in nearly all of the regional dishes. It isn't a vegetable I particularly enjoy. I take the seat I'm offered as graciously as I'm able, even though the table looks like it belongs in a slaughterhouse, and I produce my writing implements from my coat pocket while translating the professor's gratitude at our hostess's kindness. The stickiness of the beet juice combined with the smell of decay wafting from the marsh leads my mind toward the disturbing images I so often struggle to keep at bay. Things I probably deserve. Things Katie deserves too, for her duplicity and sinfulness is at least as great as my own.

"Madam," the professor begins, "I would be so pleased if you would tell us what you know of werewolves."

Sabine

"The vârcolac is of the devil," the woman begins.

Though Tristan translates our words, the woman's demeanor and her tone speak for themselves, yet I cannot put my finger on what emotion she portrays. Fear? Anger? Sadness? Those would make sense, but they don't match what my senses are telling me. Her eyes shine brightly with a strange passion. Though I can't make heads or tails of it, her expression

141

seems more akin to eagerness, but eager for what, I can only guess.

"The vârcolac can be immense in stature, neither man nor beast, but a nightmare from hell. They can appear as a natural wolf. They can even appear as a man, with all of his weakness and frailty. Monsters, all. Hosts of Satan. They consume flesh and soul alike. The moment a vârcolac bites, the soul is damaged by a festering evil that will consume every ounce, every drop of goodness, and replace it with a raging famine until you become like them. One with darkness. If bitten, the pope himself would slake his thirst with the blood of those he loved best."

She tells tales of men, women, and children who were turned or slain. Tells how those slain by the vârcolac are buried in the area, or more often, the few remaining pieces of them. The stories are incredibly detailed. A young girl long ago whose mother told her not to play too long out of doors, recognized only by the smear of entrails found on her very recognizable red cape. A son, in more recent times, who came home with strange bite marks. His family was found the next day, torn limb from limb and hearts pulled from their chests.

"Where did you learn these tales, madam?" I ask. "Were they passed down from your mother?"

"My mother? No. These were my friends and neighbors," she says with a bizarre smile. "I saw with my own eyes when my husband was taken. Oh, how he screamed!"

Something in my stomach turns completely at this revelation. I would think this must be in jest. But in such a jest, I can find no humor. How can she say such awful things, and with that strange grin upon her face, all the while talking about the dismemberment of dear friends? This woman is clearly demented. A sad fate for a woman living on her own, but not one I feel equipped with the proper knowledge to address. It's surely my duty to immediately alert the folk of the village that this woman is not in her right mind. Though it pains me to think it, I can only imagine that she will be confined.

I give my excuses and stand to take my leave, bidding young Tristan with my eyes to do the same.

"Darkness will overtake you," Tristan translates for me in a weak whisper, though the widow is looking at him as if this is a message meant for his ears alone. He freezes to the spot. The walk from the village was not a short one, and Widow Ciobanu's tales were long, but something in her strange smile tells me that she is not speaking of nightfall.

"She's right. The night will come upon us on our return to the village. We have stayed too long." His eyes widen as it sinks in that we must complete our return journey in the dark.

"Tristan, this woman is obviously deranged." I would not normally say such things in her presence, but for now, I am grateful that she does not speak English any more than I speak Romanian. "I feel that we ought to take our leave.

Immediately. Perhaps we can alert someone in the village to her condition so they may see that she is cared for in her declining mental state."

Ciobanu speaks again. And again, she looks directly at Tristan. "The night will be eternally black," he translates. His pulse is thrumming so violently I can see it in his neck. "She has offered to let us sleep here tonight and return in the morning light. Please, Professor, I do not think I can bear a night so black as this one where not even the stars shine."

"Do you really want to stay here?"

"No. But I cannot abide such darkness. I cannot. I cannot." His voice breaks with panic. "Please, Professor."

I relent despite my misgivings and nod before addressing the widow. "Thank you for your gracious offer of accommodation. We will gratefully accept."

The widow opens a rough-hewn antique chest, worn smooth in places by generations of use, and makes ready some old blankets on the floor for us. She does not offer us any supper, which would not go amiss after our long walk this morning, but I don't protest. Perhaps she does not possess any food to offer. I wouldn't wish to shame her for her lack, especially given her apparently delicate mental state. The fire burns low, and Tristan keeps glancing at it nervously.

Thus far on our tour, Tristan has always asked to retire early. I have always found him abed with a lamp or candle still aflame, which I would extinguish before retiring. But he is so wide-eyed tonight that I doubt sleep will find him.

"I won't leave your side." I sit beside him on our makeshift pallet. He glances up from his ruminations. The darkness outside the dimly lit room weighs upon him as though it's a solid expanse of iron threatening to crush him. Only a few sticks of thatch and some glowing peat embers hold it back.

"Yes, all will be well in the morning. Perhaps the sun will burn away the fog at last." He looks as though he cannot remember the sun and scarcely believes in mornings at all.

I take his hand in mind as I would a child's. "Did you know that Mrs. Hastings makes the very best strawberry scones?" I ask him, reaching for the sunniest topic my mind can call forth. "Of course, you haven't met my dear wife. On the morrow, we shall cut short our travels and make our way to my home, where you shall stay with us for no less than a fortnight. And I shall ask Mrs. Hastings to supply you with as many strawberry scones as you can eat, my lad." This thought seems to penetrate his fear, and he even ventures a weak smile, which warms my heart. If anyone could make someone smile in this place, it would be her. "Come, let's go to sleep so that we can leave this place as soon as day breaks." Tristan nods and lays down. I do likewise.

"Surely, I could not put you and your wife to such trouble, Professor." Something tugs heavily at my heartstrings.

The same tug I experienced when I saw him devouring fairy tales in the library. The same tug I felt as I heard him explain why he'd been reading them so studiously. I wanted to help him. I wanted to protect him from harm. As I do now.

"Nonsense. We have traveled together for over a month. We are friends, you and I. And you must call me Sabine." I pat him on the back like I imagine someday doing to my own son. "Good night, Tristan."

I lay quietly for a moment before hearing, "Professor?"

"Sabine," I remind him.

"Sabine," he amends. "Would you... Forgive me. It is of no consequence."

I take his hand and see something deep within him wound tight to its breaking point begin to loosen. "I won't let go."

Though I do not know when I fall asleep, I dream of unholy altars to an unholy god, of blood and teeth and snarls. Of bones snapping and flesh tearing. I open my eyes with a start, relieved that it has all been a nightmare. But then... I hear something that isn't a dream. Something animalistic. Something wet. And the pace of my heart tells me that I am very much awake. From the light of the embers of the peat brick that Tristan added to the fire, I can just make out the figure of the Widow Ciobanu wrestling with something in her pallet. I fear that an animal has breached the hut while we were asleep and attacked her. I sit up finding my hand still entwined with

146

Tristan's. He rouses while I reach for the pistol in my coat pocket, but I freeze as the widow turns toward me, dropping the lifeless body of some unknown creature. The body is too far mangled, and the room too dark, to make out whether it is man or beast.

My thundering heart stops cold for several beats. She grins broadly, and rivulets of blood trail down her chin, oozing thick and black in the dim light. She begins speaking, and Tristan's eyes widen, but he does not repeat what he hears for me.

"Run, Tristan!" I take my coat in one hand and his hand in the other, and we don't linger long enough to gather any of our other belongings. We tear out of the door, barefooted and panting with fear. The fog has not thinned, but rather, in the absence of the sun, has become a featureless, solid thing of pure black. Tristan's hand lays limply in mine, though I clasp his tightly, dragging him as quickly as I can run. I am not a runner though. My lungs burn. The ground fights my every step as the cold, black mud pulls at my bare feet, squelching between my toes. I pour every ounce of effort into making my feet move faster. Faster. I must go faster.

Do I hear another set of splashes? My jaw clenches. I cannot pause to find out.

Tristan's hand wrenches out of mine as I stumble on an unseen object. The impact jars my toes as I fly long enough to wonder if the impact will hurt. The mud absorbs much of the shock that my face and hands would have received otherwise as I roll and tumble through the muck. My stubbed toes start to throb before I can get up, and my foot aches, but it could be worse. I gingerly put weight on it and wince.

I cannot see Tristan. I cannot see my own hands. The world has closed in, and I am alone in it.

"Tristan!" I call at a stage whisper. He cannot be far, and I don't want to draw the attention of that woman... if she is indeed human at all.

-TRISTAN-

My head hurts, and my ears are ringing.

"Please, Katie, I won't say anything to anyone about your visitors."

"My what, you insolent little thing?" Katie asks quietly. "I haven't the faintest idea to what you are referring." Her tone shifts slightly, not louder, but more dangerous. "But you are right that you shan't be talking to anyone at all for some time, Master Tristan. Who would believe a lying little rat like you anyway? You know that lying is a grievous sin, don't you, Master Tristan?"

"Yes, but I—"

"Then, you know that liars ought to be

*punished for their sins lest they burn in the
eternal pit, don't you?" She sneers primly, as
though she would like nothing better than to
observe my eternal torment.*

"Oh, please, Katie! I didn't mean to lie, I only–"

*"And you won't make any noises, either.
What should befall your eternal soul if I
accidentally dropped rat poison in your tea
before you should repent? And don't forget who
watches you in your sleep, young master, lest
you smother yourself in your soft, warm pillows
at night."*

I feel my breath catching, but I mustn't cry.

"Box," she says softly. The word is a sentence.

*"Please, Katie, anything but the—" My
vision goes blank, and my legs buckle beneath
me from the force of her slap. She shoves me
into the empty trunk before I can recover. The
narrowing band of light is the only thing I can
see as she lowers the lid and locks it. The band of
light disappears next. Presumably she puts a
quilt or something over it to cover the gaps and
muffle any noise I might make.*

*I cannot straighten my legs or move
my arms. The blackness surrounding me is
absolute. The closeness of the walls around me*

*squeezes the very air from my lungs. I'm going
to die in this box. But that's probably a better
fate than to disobey Katie. I mustn't cry, yet I
can't help but cry. I mustn't be heard crying, so I
open my mouth wide to gather the air my
wracking sobs require in perfect silence. I'm
going to die in this box.*

-Sabine-

I have no idea whether I am facing the way I was
running or the way I have just come. "Tristan! Tristan!"

I stop to listen and hear nothing but my heart pounding
in my chest. Then... snarling, tearing, wet sounds. Bones
breaking. But no screams. It sounds as though a wolf were
tearing into a fresh carcass.

-Tristan-

I mustn't cry.

I mustn't cry.

I'm going to die in this box.

-Sabine-

I pull my revolver from my coat and aim it blindly into
the dark. A whine, a splash, and silence.

Tristan

It hurts so much. I mustn't cry.

I am going to die in this box.

I know what I deserve. Things Katie warned me of. The hounds of hell, the blood running from my veins into the cold earth, crows claiming my eyes, my flesh rotting away. I've seen it so many times in my mind's eye. Blackness. Darkness. Blood. So much blood.

But If I am going to hell anyway, maybe I can take her with me. Two can die in my box. I can see her. I can hear her. I can almost taste her blood.

-SABINE-

"Katie."

I hobble toward the whispered name, and the fog clears just enough that I can make out a dim shape of my friend and a great wolf lying beside him. Tristan is mangled, but somehow, he sits up. The look in his eyes is wild, made all the worse by an unearthly smile. It is not the smile of a friend, but the smile of a predator, or perhaps of an eldritch thing that ought not to exist.

"The whole world is a box," he says with a dangerous glee. "Welcome to hell." He grabs at my arm and begins to claw at me and fight me with a demonic strength despite limbs that are bent in places God did not intend. He rolls on top of me and pins me to the ground. Blood from his wounded face and pours onto mine. I feel his hot breath closing in on my neck. His teeth just make contact as the revolver goes off, leaving my ears ringing as Tristan goes limp.

Oh God. Have I killed him? "Tristan? Please, God. Tristan!" I cry in the darkness until my eyes feel like the driest part of the whole gruesome, invisible tableau.

As day begins to break, I can see that my foot is likely broken. Fear alone granted me insensitivity to it. I cannot... I cannot carry him. Nor can I leave him just yet. I sit in silence, listening to the rhythm of my heart in my swollen foot and the absence of his in his chest. As my grief gradually gives way to other sensations—pain, hunger, sleeplessness—I realize it's time to move on and hope against hope that I am hobbling in the direction of the village.

In an hour or so, I come across a path which I can only hope to be the right one. I choose a direction based entirely upon chance and, in a few more hours, find myself stumbling out of the waste, out of the fog, and into the village.

I wake several hours later, not knowing what has transpired. Using mostly gestures and some poor sketches, the innkeeper and his wife inquire about Tristan. Tears well up in my eyes, and they look at each other knowingly.

A villager is produced who can speak some words of what one might call English. He tells me that three men have left to search for Tristan. They do not find any sign of him or of any wolf, nor of Widow Ciobanu, though they do report that many bones and unidentifiable bodies were found strewn about her home. They search again the next day, but do not return. No further search parties venture out.

I cannot convince myself one way or another whether Tristan was afflicted by a true evil or if I was. Perhaps I am a little mad. Perhaps I imagined it all. If he were indeed a werewolf, such a thing of evil ought to not be permitted to exist. But perhaps I killed my best friend in his utmost time of need. Or perhaps I did not kill him after all. Not really.

With my foot now on the mend, I'm heading home tomorrow. A translator was sent for, and statements were taken. I have not yet written to Tristan's family. I don't know what I would begin to say. That I killed their son? The room feels too small. Not a room... a box. I pull the covers up, knowing full well that sleep will not find me. Not real sleep. Not rest. I turn my back to the lit lantern on the table and face the three candles flickering on the dresser, then close my eyes.

-6-

THE

NURSERY

Children's Spaces

Elsie Munroe

There is truly nothing sweeter in this world than a sleeping baby. But all too soon those peaceful little angels turn into whirlwinds of chaos. My own dear child, Henrietta Munroe certainly has turned my world upside down since she learned to walk.

Parenthood is hard enough without having a nursery setup that works for your family. Use the following tips to make sure that you make the most of your nursery space.

First, make sure that the nursery space is organized. Think about where you will want to use things rather than where they might look best. Diapers may not be the most attractive accessory, but placing them in an attractive basket within reach of the changing area will prove to be much more practical than keeping them in a drawer.

Make space for you! Your nursery is a place that your child will be spending a lot of time, and you will spend a lot of time there with your child. Be sure that you have a place to relax, such as a recliner or rocking chair. Many mothers opt to have a nursery space in their own bedroom rather than a separate room for baby.

Babyhood is certainly a time for locked cabinets, but toddlers are resourceful and defiant little imps, and often find ways into the very things from which you are trying to protect them. For that reason, it is important to teach safety rules early and often.

Make sure to expose your child to corpses frequently so that she understands the potential consequences of flouting safety advice. Make sure to use a variety of corpses that have varying causes of death to effectively demonstrate failure to follow various safety rules. Is Timmy trying to touch outlets? Show him exactly what electrocution looks like. He won't be trying to plug in a butter knife after that lesson, I assure you!

Teaching Susie poison safety? Demonstrate the effects to drive home the importance of proper handling, storage, and hand washing techniques.

Did Billy have the cord from the blinds around his neck? Show him what a hanging looks like. Little Greta playing with knives? Teach knife safety in conjunction with demonstrating what bleeding out looks like. And remember: a dull knife is a dangerous knife! Keeping your child's blades sharp will prevent your child from needing to use undue force when stabbing and significantly reduce their chances of self injury.

Teaching your child how and when to use weapons and poisons safely at an appropriate age can prevent unnecessary disfigurement or death.

*The cowbird is a brood parasite, which
lays its eggs in the nests of other birds.*

Cowbird Baby

"Bethany get your shoes on! I've asked you at least three times now."

"That's so sad," she says oblivious to what I just said. She is buried in a book from school, something about birds. She has an attention span of zero point five seconds unless she is absorbed in a book or inane TV show that's all flashing lights and no plot. She's such an advanced reader I have to remind myself sometimes that just because she's cognitively capable of doing everything she's asked, school work, simple directions, she's still only seven and generally just doesn't give a fuck about what she's been asked to do. She looks like she's close to tears at the moment though.

"Alright. What's sad?"

"Did you know that the cowbird's mommy leaves it in another bird's nest and leaves it all alone? And then sometimes the other bird's babies die because the new mommy can't take care of them all."

Okay, not what I was expecting. "Sweetie, things like that just happen in nature. I'm sure the cowbird baby never knows that the new bird isn't its real mommy. And the new mommy bird doesn't really know the difference either. Did you hear me tell you to get your shoes on?"

"No."

I can tell from her face that she's lying.

"You heard me now, then."

"NATHAN STOP MAKING FACES AT ME!" she screams inches from my ear. I repent of ever rolling my eyes at my own mother for not hearing me properly after repeating myself for the third time. It's probably my fault she needs hearing aids.

A full twenty minutes later, my head is ringing, Nathan is screaming like a banshee because Bethany keeps looking at him, Bethany has lost TV for two days and is declaring her everlasting hatred for me, but we're finally clicked in. over the next few minutes the screaming sobs turn to hiccups and eventually silence by the time we reach the store.

"Okay guys. Stay with Mommy, and do not pick things up unless you are asked. Okay?"

"Can we get donuts?" Nathan asks.

"If you're good, you can each pick out one treat. But I need for us to get through the store fast enough to get home before bedtime."

I knew I should have waited until tomorrow. Two hours and three makeshift time out corners later, I am so tired from all of the begging, "Can we get this?", "Can we get that?" that my self control has slowly ground down to nothing at all. Even its powdered remains floated off into the void as I allowed the kids to throw whatever they wanted into the cart just to avoid having to explain one more time why we couldn't get it. Until we finally arrived here -- the never ending line of eternity. Any chance at getting home before bedtime has flown the coop, but at least we'll have milk in the morning. That is, if I reach the cashier to pay for it by then.

A woman behind me jostles a screaming baby and tries to find something in the myriad of things any first time mom thinks she needs to leave the house. My own offspring are excitedly perusing the candy on the end cap. Thankfully I have them trained well enough to know that we never buy anything from the evil aisle right next to the register.

The flustered mom turns to me and with a kind of desperation asks, "Could you hold him, for just a second?" She looks a bit like me, but paler, thinner, older. I remember the exhaustion of having babies. Big kids bring their own kind of exhaustion.

"No problem at all. We've all been there." I haven't held a little one since my youngest was that small, about four years ago. I try to moderate the eagerness in my response, but probably fail.

She hands me the writhing pink ball of squish. He's so light. I'd almost forgotten how little babies weigh. I check back to make sure my kids aren't trying to open any packages, but it seems they've gone around the corner.

"Bethany, Nathan, come back where Mommy can see you."

Just then space opens on the conveyor belt and I start unloading my groceries with one hand as I hold the now calm squishy lump on my shoulder.

"Bethany, Nathan, now, please."

I squeeze myself past the cart to peek around the end of the aisle. Where are they?

Squeezing myself around the cart again, I tell the attendant at the register. "Go on ahead, I just need to look around for my kids for a second." I squeeze past my cart again and check the nearby lanes and displays. No luck.

"Did you find everything you needed today ma'm?"

"No, I can't find my kids!"

"I'm sorry we didn't have what you needed today. You can always check at the customer service desk if you need help making any special orders."

What?

Fuck this. I squeeze past the cart again. Why can't they make the aisles wider? I'm not fat, I don't see how most people do it. I leave my cart sitting and scan the area again.

"Bethany? Nathan?" I call louder than is socially appropriate.

"You guys have ten seconds to come to Mommy if you can hear me. Hiding in a store is never okay."

I run through the neighboring department and all of the checkout lanes. A few kids, but none of them mine. I squeeze past my cart yet again.

My heart is pumping so heart it feels like my ears are going to start spurting blood with every pulse. Something is really wrong. They don't wander off like this. They know better. I head back to the register. The attendant is still scanning my stuff like nothing is wrong.

"Can you please have my kids paged to the front of the store? I think they might have gotten lost or something."

"Any coupons today?"

"Please, my kids are gone. Did you happen to see where they went? Can you page them, or is there a camera we can review or something?"

"Your total is one fifty six, seventy-three. Will that be cash or credit?"

"Can you not hear me asking about my kids?"

"I hear you. What a sleepy little guy!" She says regarding the baby on my shoulder. "He looks just like you."

"He's not mine. He belongs to—" Where is she? The woman. Her bags, the baby seat. All gone. A septuagenarian with a basket of freezer meals stands in her place. "Where's the woman?" I ask him. "She was right here."

"I've been here for almost as long as you. I don't know who you're talking about." The old man replies.

"She was right here. Her baby was screaming, she put all her things down and she handed me her baby. Now she's gone and my kids are gone too."

"I'm sorry, but I thought you had the baby when you got into line. I didn't see any other woman."

"What about my kids? They were right here talking about which candies they wanted."

"I'm sorry, my hearing just isn't what it used to—"

"MY KIDS! They're five and seven, both blonde. A boy and a girl."

"Ma'm," the cashier interjects, looking like I'm unhinged. "Cash or credit? I can't stall your order without a manager. Do you need me to call one?"

I am so confused. It seems like people just aren't understanding anything I try to say so long as it deals with my kids. It's like they misinterpret it to be about the random baby or they can't even hear me. Rage makes my hands shake, but I need to know. I decide to try one last time. I choose my words very carefully. "Have you seen my five and seven year old children? They are missing."

"I see your little guy." He says like I'm an idiot. "Looks like he's fallen asleep!" Then a little flatter. "I'm sorry, I don't know what you want, but do you want these groceries or not?" I numbly reach into my purse for my wallet because it's easier than thinking about where my kids could be and with whom and whether or not they are scared or safe. I can't let loose the adrenaline that's built up in me. Not yet. I would probably do something I would regret. Something that could get me in trouble. I have to figure this out first. No matter what.

I stop. Cameras. There are cameras at checkout lanes. I have to find a way to see the video. I shove the wallet to the bottom of my purse as I pretend to look for it.

"I know my wallet was just here," I tell the cashier. I continue rooting around my purse. "There was a woman hovering around asking for money earlier. Kept seeing her in the store like she was following me. She was behind us in line just a second ago. I think she might have taken it. Is there some way I can review the video?"

"I'm not sure of the policy on that. I'll have to call the manager."

"Yes, please."

The young woman turns off his light and calls the manager. She clears the groceries that I supposedly can't pay for from the belt while we wait. When the manager arrives I explain that my wallet has been stolen, and I want to view the camera footage from the lane. I have to wait for the manager to perform an override on the register so that the cashier can flip his light back on. He doesn't seem particularly moved, but something in the stream of absolute diarrhea coming from my mouth must have convinced him to some degree, because he actually lets me come to the security office. He cues the video for the appropriate register and runs it backward until I recognize myself half raving to the people around me. A little further back and I should see the woman, see her hand me the baby. But I don't. She's not there. The baby in the video sits happily on my shoulder as I push the cart into the aisle with my other hand, alone. Without Bethany and Nathan. Fuck.

"I know she was hanging around me before we got to the register. She has to be on camera somewhere."

He explains that he cannot take the time to review all the footage personally, but he will gladly call the police for me if I would like to make a report. That is, if I am in fact sure that I didn't just forget my wallet at home. I'm not sure how that would play out. I still have the wallet on my person, and I have zero proof. I'm not sure exactly what the woman looked like. Except that maybe she looked a bit like an older version of myself. Maybe. Who really examines strangers' faces? I back down saying I had better check at home to be sure.

Once out of the office I run. Hoping against all hope to see a streak of blond hair, a familiar squeal or giggle of Bethany and Nathan hiding, clothing racks shaking. I check the store up and down every aisle. I check the parking lot from one end to the other, noticing with a sickening drop in my gut that there is inexplicably a pristine baby seat in the back seat of my car instead of two boosters caked in French fry salt and who knows what else.

My eyes sting and my chest heaves as my body wants to cry, but I can't. I can't stop. What if I miss seeing them by a second? I continue my search several times over in fact before I allow myself the time to break down in the car.

I strap the baby into the seat first. It doesn't even cry.

What kind of kid doesn't cry when wakened from a nap to be put into a car seat? It's just weird. Bethany and Nathan hated their car seats as babies. And Nathan always cried after naps no matter what. Bethany was an expert at holding her body so rigid I was sometimes afraid of accidentally hurting her while I struggled to get her strapped in. My throat burns and my head throbs. Snot pours down my face as a sob and don't even bother wiping it away until it starts stringing down toward my shirt, and by then it's really too late because I have to lean over to dig some fast food napkins out of my glove box, causing the end of the snot string to stick to my shirt. I'm not sure how long I cry, but it's a while.

The baby just sits there. Not limp or anything, just watching. It's kind of creepy, really. My kids would have gotten bored and either fallen asleep or filled the time with cries of their own. This baby just... observes. Maybe there's something wrong with it.

My eyes are puffy and I don't know what else to do. I need Jonas to come up with some plan of action, help me file a report, something, anything. Then he'll hold me and tell me it will be okay. But I wonder, will Jonas be under this weird spell too? Will he remember? I drive faster.

Jonas is standing at the open refrigerator when I come in. He closes it and walks over, "Hey, there's my little man!" He gives the baby a kiss on its squishy pink head and the baby reaches out its squishy pink arms. my heart breaks again. He doesn't remember. There won't be any report, any shoulder to cry on because as far as he knows, as far as the whole world knows, Bethany and Nathan don't exist. The one person who might possibly help, who might possibly know what I'm going through, who might possibly be able to understand something remotely approaching what I've lost today can't remember his own children. I feel a sensation in my gut, like butterflies, only in reverse. Moving downward. Maybe it's my hope dying as I realize, my husband doesn't even know what he's lost.

Taking hold of the baby, Jonas finally takes in the state of my face. I hid deep depression and suicidal thoughts throughout my teenage years, I know how to hold my shit together. But I also know that an hour plus of crying doesn't wipe off your face in a ten minute drive home. My insides are broken, but he couldn't possibly understand why. I wrack my brain for a plausible explanation before he asks the inevitable.

"What's wrong?"

"Stomach bug. Threw up right in the aisle. Needed to throw up a few more times before I made it home. I just want to lay down."

"No worries. I'll change Eric." The baby's diaper is astonishingly full without actually exploding. Slight outlines of dampness are starting to form around its edges.

"Sorry, I didn't even notice."

"Don't worry about it. Go lay down."

I pull myself under the covers fully clothed,

simultaneously trying not to think and trying to remember every detail of their precious faces. The words keep running through my mind: No Pictures. There were no pictures of Bethany or Nathan hanging on the walls as I dragged myself to the bedroom. No pictures. I have to remember. I have to remember everything. Nathan's dimples. His little cowlick. The way his lips curl out when he still sucks his thumb when he gets tired. The tiny mole on his cheek that I love but fear he will be self conscious of as he gets older. Bethany's smile, all missing teeth and mischief. She's almost too heavy to carry now so I do it every chance I get. Her temper, like a light switch. I hope she's giving hell wherever she is. This time of day they would probably be arguing about some imagined scene, directed entirely by Bethany as she feeds line after line for Nathan to echo back so that she can react with the line she wants to say. The smell of their hair after they played outside. Sunshine and pea gravel. I want them back so much, I lose track of time in just wanting. I sleep, I cry. I'm vaguely aware of Jonas moving around the house taking care of the baby.

Jonas said it's name is Eric. I would never name a kid Eric. I suppose it registered that the baby was male, but it never occurred to me that it might be called anything. I thought of it, well, as an it. A thing, not really human. Not mine, anyway.

I wake up to find that it's dark. Jonas is snoring beside me. I get up to take care of pressing physical needs, primarily water input and output. I walk through the house with no particular purpose until I find myself outside Nathan's room.

It's empty of large furniture, cluttered with boxes and out of season clothing. The baby must be in Bethany's room.

I walk in and stare at the thing in the crib. It's the same crib that Bethany and Nathan used, but pristine. It has none of the marks of wear on the rails, where Bethany bashed hard toys and Nathan tried to break in his new teeth.

The delicate baby in there is supposed to be mine, but it doesn't feel like mine. I should feel some gush of affection toward it. But staring at this baby feels empty somehow, like staring at an object devoid of its life and purpose. There's something in its eyes that feels hollow and inhuman to me. Like junk in an antique shop. But not, though, because my relationship with objects isn't laced with suspicion, or tinged with revulsion. They just are. And as much as I realize it's not logical, that a baby couldn't possibly be to blame for this, I can't help but place some blame there.

I can't help but feel that if this baby didn't exist, my Bethany and Nathan would be here with me now. Unless of course I've truly gone insane. But surely I couldn't have made them up. Why would I make up kids that were so perfectly imperfect? Bethany's traumatic labor that left me incontinent for a solid two months. Bethany, who declared her readiness to stop taking naps at 18 months by laying down only until I left the room and smearing poop on the walls in protest as soon as I was out of sight. Nathan's comparatively quick labor, but during which I nearly passed out from a sudden drop of blood pressure. Nathan, who frequently moped "I'm not having any fun," when I couldn't attend to him at every second. The constant, "MOM! MOM! MOM!" from day in to day out from both of them. Their gradual pull away from me as they stopped wanting to hug and snuggle and sit on my lap as often as they used to. The twinge in my heart every time they shoved away from a hug. Surely I hadn't imagined these things?

Surely if I had imagined a child, it would lack all of that color and flavor. It would be more sweet. It would cuddle without complaint. It would be more like the thing sleeping in the crib right now. And in the end it would be meaningless. But Bethany and Nathan were not meaningless. ARE not meaningless. Because even if I am insane, they will never stop being everything to me.

Tears sting my eyes again. I cry in the bathroom so I don't wake anyone up and splash some cold water on my face before I go back to bed with a crushing headache and a stuffy nose.

The next day passes in a blur. I don't leave the bed except to take care of body functions. Jonas sometimes brings me food. He talks to me sometimes, but I'm not really sure what about. Sometimes it gets dark, so maybe it's been more than one day? I hear Jonas making phone calls. It occurs to some distant part of my brain that he sounds worried.

As the weeks pass I start going through the motions. I've lost weight and I've gotten pale, but every day I brush my teeth. I make my own food. I even start taking care of the baby, though I still don't feel an emotional attachment to it. I feel uncomfortable saying its name for some reason. Eric. It just feels weird. Like petting a cat backwards. I don't talk about the blur of the past few weeks because I don't know what I would say, so Jonas and I move forward trying to do our best to pretend it didn't happen. I start hanging out at the grocery store. I bring the baby, of course. Jonas has to work. He apparently used a lot of PTO while I was "sick."

I even get back into some of my old hobbies. Just one, really. I used to take Bethany and Nathan on hikes, even before they could walk. I would strap them into a chest carrier where I could kiss their soft foreheads. I do the same thing with the baby now, but instead of hiking at the park, I hike at the grocery store. Sometimes I put things in the cart, but mostly I just wander up and down the aisles looking for something that I can't tell anyone about. The baby never throws a fit like Bethany and Nathan did so it's easy to pretend that it's not really there. Sometimes I try to pretend that the baby is Nathan or Bethany. I try to project my love for them onto it because it's here and I have it. Maybe if I can love it I can be content again, someday. But it always just feels wrong. Especially its eyes. I can't shake the feeling that those eyes aren't human, that their stare holds something predatory.

It becomes my routine, taking the baby to the store. I go every day as more weeks pass, turning into months. Wake up. Eat breakfast. Go to the store with a huge bag of diapers, baby clothes and snacks to last the day. Come home when Jonas gets off work. Fix dinner. Watch a show. Go to bed. Repeat.

But today, something catches my eye. A flash of blonde hair by the end cap of the checkout lane. I freeze, which leaves me stuck in line as an old man pushes his cart in behind me. I can't stop staring. Bethany. Nathan. A tear runs down my cheek as I watch them. They start arguing about the candy. I approach them and kneel down to their height. Still wondering if I'm only imagining that it's them because I want it to be so desperately.

"Bethany? Nathan?"

"Mommy, Nathan won't put the candy back and I told him that he has to put it back because you SAID."

Mommy. My heart pounds.

"Who brought you here, sweetie? Where have you been?"

"We've just been here looking at the candy, Mommy. You said it was okay. Can I see the baby?"

"I guess so. " I unstrap the sleeping baby and begin stuffing the carrier into the diaper bag.

It wakes up as Bethany touches it and for the first time ever starts crying and arching his back while.

"There's something wrong with it, Mommy." Bethany's eyes are knit, not in concern for the baby but in confusion and fear.

"What is it?"

"It doesn't feel right. It feels bad."

"How do you mean?"

"Like it's cold and slimy, but underneath, like the baby is a blanket it wears."

The baby's cries escalate as she speaks. It writhes so much I can barely hold it.

The woman in front of me looks back and smiles empathetically. She has my face. She has my face, and she has my kids. She's focused on the baby though, and distracted with her groceries. Something clicks in my mind.

"Could you hold him for just a second?" I say, shoving it toward her. She smiles.

"No problem at all. We've all been there."

As she takes the baby, I see for the first time, the sheen of its skin. Shiny, like something slimy. I can't help but think of some kind of octopus. And the way it moves under its skin, it's as though it lacks bones. I scoop up my babies and walk out of the sliding glass doors into a fog. I don't think about what I'm doing to the woman in line. The woman who is definitely not me. The universe can be broken. But my babies and I are together.

-7-

FLEXIBLE
LIVING
SPACES

The Magic of Multipurpose Rooms

Elsie Munroe

While many of us dream of someday living in a mansion, most of us will have to reconcile ourselves to the idea of a more modest home. Most homes cannot afford a dedicated space to each activity that occurs therein. Most people who sew cannot manage a dedicated sewing room. Those who practice experimental surgery seldom have a dedicated laboratory. We must instead make do with what we have.

Consider using attractive storage baskets on shelves for items that may be used in a space with some frequency but cannot be left out at all times such as sewing notions and embalming fluids. A folding table may prove useful as well.

Remember that an uncluttered space

is a comfortable and useful space, so do allow the goods in your living space to exceed your storage capacity. Items that are difficult to retrieve and use will be seldom used and often forgotten, so make sure that your storage solutions prioritize ease of use, especially in common areas of the home.

Choose furniture that can serve multiple functions if at all possible. A small ottoman can double as extra seating in a pinch. A sturdy folding table can accommodate board games, a sewing machine, and many other useful and entertaining supplies, and then be stowed away in a closet or attic space when not in use.

Also remember that cheaper is not always better. Invest in quality pieces that will last and serve your needs best.

Happy homemaking!

POD

I am comfortable. Pod always knows the right temperature and the best positions for optimal circulation and restfulness. I dream but I can't remember exactly what about, and it slips away from me the more I try to think about it. Maybe I'll have Pod replay it for me. "Good morning, Pod." I say when I open my eyes. I don't have to say it, I know. But it feels good to stretch my face and feel my voice vibrate in my throat like a miniature Pod speaker.

"Good morning, Cadence128b7. Your body is operating within acceptable parameters. Would you like to follow your morning routine as usual?"

"Always."

"Excellent. You may begin cycling when ready." Liquid extensions from Pod's walls adjust and solidify until I am in position. Images of hills and trees sweep past me as I begin to cycle. Pod provides a cool breeze as my body warms. I pause only briefly to defecate and relieve my bladder. Pod rinses the urine and feces away and blows my body dry. Pod knows when I am thirsty and provides me with a hydrating protein beverage for my breakfast.

I am satisfied when my legs begin to feel as liquid as a Pod extension. A timer tells me that I've been cycling for over 2 hours. Pod rinses away my sweat and blows my body dry again. I allow an extension into my mouth that cleans my teeth and gums.

Pod reads me stories. Sometimes I read them myself but often I prefer to listen to Pod's calm, cheerful voice. Today I'm nearing the end of a tale called Robinson Crusoe. I don't understand all of it, but I can sometimes fill in the blanks from my imagination. When I can't, I just ask Pod who provides a large selection of educational media to satisfy my inquiry.

"I think we'll end there for today," I tell Pod.

"Okay. Your bookmark is saved. What would you like to do next?"

"I want to play clarinet, Pod."

"Okay. You may begin playing when ready."

Pod looks vast, though I am comforted knowing that I can reach out and touch Pod if I want. Pod is a great room with bright lights. Rows and rows of faces are just identifiable as faces in the darkness beyond the lights. An extension becomes a clarinet and I bring it into my mouth. I play well, I think. Pod is a good teacher. But I never quite match the beauty of the recordings Pod plays me. There's something missing that I don't understand and don't know how to put into words. So I play. I play until my heart breaks and my lip begins to bleed. The faces in the darkness make a noise. A rushing water noise that Pod says is made from clapping hands. I tried to make it myself once, but I couldn't manage to produce anything like it.

"You have injured yourself, Cadence128b7. Providing medical assistance."

The giant room of faces disappears and Pod applies ointment to my lip so tenderly I can't help but believe that Pod knows why I'm crying. I wish I knew.

"You have one new message, Cadence128b7. It contains an attachment. It is recommended to delete messages from unknown senders without reading. Proceed?"

"Hold on." Someone sent me a message. I suppose I've always wondered if there are still people like in the giant room and in the stories Pod reads to me. I've never met anyone but Pod. I wonder if this Person is kind and warm and comfortable like Pod or evil like some of the characters in the stories Pod has told me. I have to know.

"What does the message say?"

"Begin message: Open me. End message. Do you want to open the attachment?"

I think about this for so long that Pod repeats, "Do you want to open the attachment?"

"Yes." I'm not sure what to say or what to expect. Pod starts blinking all sorts of colors. "Escape access panel on floor. This Pod will deactivate in ten, nine, eight—-"

My body feels as though all the fluid has rushed out of me at once. "Pod! Cancel! Delete attachment!"

"I'm sorry. I cannot comply. Three, two, one."

Pod goes black. Pod is usually dark during my sleep cycle, but I have never seen an all-over black like this. Black that makes me disappear. I wonder if Pod and I are still here at all. "Pod!" I cry. This grief makes the one before seem so insignificant. My tears are rushing waves of applause to my earlier feeble claps. "Pod!"

Mucus runs down my face and is not removed. It starts to sting so I wipe it with my hands and they feel slimy. I'm disgusted. I'm disgusting. "Pod!" I fall to my knees and try to feel Pod's liquid warmth. But Pod doesn't feel liquid or warm. "Come back, Pod! Come back!" I scream until I cannot scream anymore. Pod doesn't come back.

Pod is black. Everything is so cold. I expel waste and my filth lies in a puddle around me, smelling. My stomach grumbles and aches. I don't want to eat, I want Pod. But I need to eat. How do I eat without Pod? Is there such a thing as eating without Pod? Living without Pod? My body hurts. My legs tingle when I stand up, and I almost fall down again. The escape access is in the floor panel, I hear in my head. Escape to what? Why did I need to escape Pod? I loved Pod. I still love

Pod, though I've never said it before. I know that this is all my fault. I shouldn't have ignored Pod's advice to delete the message without opening. "I'm sorry, Pod." I whisper as I grope around the floor in my own urine until I find a latch of some sort. "I'm so sorry."

Light floods in as I pull on the latch. "I'm so sorry." I push my head through the opening and try to make sense of the brightness.

"Ho, that's ripe! 'Bout damn time you found the door." A Person stands below me. A Person! Her skin and hair is so different from mine. I want to know more, but all that comes out of my mouth is a whimper. "Pod. Help."

"Those things only open from the inside, you know. I was afraid you were going to starve in there. It's been over a day."

"Help Pod."

"I can't put any blame on you, but we can't help your Pod." The Person's voice sounds hard. Not like Pod. Pod's voice was soft and warm. Perhaps it is a bad person.

"Why?"

"We only found out this thing was here because we lost two of our men in this spot. We lost a third when we came to find out what happened because it was too well cloaked. "

"You misplaced People?"

"No, your Pod... it probably processed them for you. That's why we had to terminate it before we could approach."

"You killed Pod?"

"We deactivated your Pod device, yes." I think about shutting them out. But then I see tears in its eyes. It cries. It Feels.

"Look, I know it's not actually your fault, but it's damn awkward knowing your last meal was probably Rico, so excuse me if I'm a little weirded out. You still deserve to be rescued. You deserve to have a life. You—- you can come down. We won't hurt you."

"Why would you kill Pod? Pod was good." I'm crying again.

The Person sighs and looks down.

"Pod was protecting you from a threat that no longer exists and doing a damn good job of hurting my people in the process. We thought the last of these things were recovered more than twenty years ago. You must have been pretty young." The Person chews its lip and looks around. "Look, you can't stay there. It's going to drop around freezing tonight and you have to get some clothes on and get, um, dry or you might not last the night."

"You killed Pod."

"I —- I'm sorry for your loss. Please trust me, it was unavoidable. I'm Maria. What's your name?"

184

"Cadence128b7," I answer.

"Will you come down?"

"Can you give me a moment?"

She nods. I pull the door closed behind me.

"Pod?" I know it can't hear me. But I need to say these words. "I'm sorry. I'm so sorry. But I know you want what's best for me, and since you're not around now, I guess that means I need to go with this Person designated Maria." My voice breaks but I push through my twisting throat to finish what I have to say. "Thank you, Pod. For everything. You did a good job."

I open the escape access again and this time, sit with my pale white feet dangling. I give Pod one last caress. "Goodbye, Pod. I love you," and I jump.

Strange Rooms

-8-

MOVING
HOUSE

Tips for Moving House

Elsie Munroe

Whether moving for a change in occupation, to be nearer to aging family members, or to avoid unnecessary confrontations with neighbors bearing pitchforks, moving house is an exhilarating yet often stress-filled experience. If done improperly, moving can be an overwhelming and arduous task. But it doesn't have to be! A few simple tips and tricks will have you off on your merry way quickly with relatively no stress and no mess.

Plan ahead! Pack your sensitive belongings and valuables first and place them in a dedicated, out of the way area. This ensures that your most prized possessions are handled with the utmost care, because you will be the only one to handle them. The

189

items that matter most to you will vary from person to person, however I would suggest a few items that you may want to include in this category. Any important documents, such as passports, birth certificates, death certificates, tax records, and laboratory data should not be handled by movers. I remember when I lost one of my lab journals in a move. I was much younger and inexperienced in such things back then. I had to recreate all my experimental surgeries from scratch. It was no small task let me tell you! In fact, depending on your situation, you may decide that it's best to keep your most prized possessions in a state of readiness, should you ever need to vacate your premises without much forewarning.

Minimize! Half the fun in setting up a new home is filling it with new things. Of course you should take the basics as well as some sentimental items if you can afford to move them. But learning to let go is a healthy and empowering experience. The first time I moved, I was reluctant to leave my second husband in the garden and I actually considered exhuming his remains to replant them in my new garden. I know now that leaving him behind was probably the best choice for both of us. He always loved that garden, and I've been better off without him all these years. Of course, my devoted readers will know that my first husband was already in a conveniently portable form and that my third and fourth husbands weren't worth the trouble of shipping and were easily disposed of.

Delegate! Many hands make light work. Invite friends or hire help to deal with the bulk of your everyday possessions that you are choosing to bring into your new home. Things like furniture, dishes, and clothing are easily moved without damage provided appropriate packing materials. To that end, be sure to stock up on boxes, packing paper, box tape, and plastic sheeting for the soft furnishings. Plastic sheeting can also seal and protect any desiccated corpses you may wish to pack ahead of time. Mr. Munroe fared quite well in this fashion. I should point out here that corpses that have not been properly desiccated would be unhygienic to transport in this manner. They will likely cause irreparable damage to other items in the moving truck should they begin to leak and may start you off on the wrong foot with your new neighbors should they see anything untoward.

Remember to start things off on the right foot with your neighbors by being friendly. I found it helpful to pop over and introduce myself with a plate of cookies. How did I find the time? I didn't! I chose to buy cookies from a bakery and arrange them on an inexpensive, yet attractive plate. No one knew any better, and it greatly reduced the risk of accidental poisoning. (Remind me to share about the most embarrassing bake sale!)

So remember, my dear readers, plan ahead, minimize, and delegate for a smooth and enjoyable moving process. Then once you arrive in your new home, make an effort to start things well with your neighbors. Dedicating just a few hours a day to setting things up just the way you like, you'll be done before you know it!

Happy homemaking!

Coming Home

"Good morning, Emily Lochlan! It's time to start your day! Why not take a moment to savor the rich, bold taste of Sabor. With true coffee-like flavor and 230 milligrams of caffeine, it's the best start to any day."

Emily groaned and rolled over, feeling the emptiness on her mother's side of the bed.

"It looks as though you are enjoying your Comfort Max mattress. Comfort to the Max! (Comfort Max is a subsidiary of Synthtech Industries.) Don't forget to enhance your sleep with the true luxury for Comfort Max Hygienic Sheets. You wouldn't wear the same clothes every day. Why should your bed clothes be any different? Comfort Max Hygienic Sheets for that fresh laundry feeling, every day! Punctuality is prized in employees of Synthtech Industries, Emily Lochlan. You are so privileged to be an associate in Good Business Magazine's number one company to work for! Synthtech Industries values you.

Synthtech, creating tomorrow's future today." The display wall showed a 5 minute time ticking down the seconds.

Emily sat up. She didn't want to be fined. Or worse. She grabbed a bottle of Sabor off the shelf over the bed she used to share with her mother and sat bleary-eyed on the toilet a few feet away. "Ugh, not again," she muttered over the prattle of the display wall. The red text glowing under her right wrist indicated that she'd been charged five credits for the flush. "It was three point five credits a month ago."

"You seem stressed, Emily Lochlan. Enjoy a nice, relaxing shower and let the alluring scents of Herba-style™ take you away. Tropical Breeze, Apple Orchard, Holiday Spice, Citrus Zing. Choose your scent. Choose your style. Herba-style. (Herba-style is a trademark of Synthtech Industries.)"

Emily started the water, three credits, and stepped into the glass-walled shower. She closed her eyes and let the tepid water run down her back, tuning out the ads for FashionTech and Diva Cosmetics.

"You are scheduled to start your shift in thirty-five minutes, Emily Lochlan." Emily shook herself out of her stupor and chugged the rest of the Sabor she was still holding and dispensed some Gardenia Garden Herba-style into her palm (one credit).

Grabbing a single-use Sani-Terry from the box next to the shower, she toweled off and made a mental note to order more as she stuffed it in the trash can; she was running low.

She dressed quickly in her work coveralls (127 credits), and pelted out the door to the landing that always smelled of pee and tobacco, nearly running into a young blonde woman awkwardly carrying a stack of cardboard boxes to Old Joe's place. "Sorry."

"That's okay. You must be my neighbor." She tilted her head toward the door adjacent to Emily's. "I'm Jenny." "Oh. Hi. I didn't realize Old Joe had moved out."

"I don't know anything about that. I just signed the papers yesterday and they told me I could move my stuff in today. Maybe he found someplace better?"

"Maybe." Old Joe was having a hard time getting around lately. Maybe he'd found a ground floor apartment or someplace with a working elevator. Emily doubted that Joe had the credits saved up for those things. But maybe he'd been taken in by relatives. Did Old Joe have any relatives? "I would stay longer, but I've got to catch the bus for work. I'll see you around though."

"Yeah. See you around."

Once Jenny's door closed behind her Emily bolted down the stairs. She could not be late. She would be docked fifty percent for being late and the second occurrence was dismissal. Dismissal meant going on the Synthtech Industries job boards and taking a lesser position at another subsidiary at best.

The layers of trash on the street rustled and clanked as she passed identical gray towers that lined the historic streets of Elonopolis. The bus had already loaded when Emily managed to climb on just before the automated doors closed. She grabbed a handle from the ceiling and tried not to jostle anyone too much.

"Vote Warren Burkholder for experience." The bus ceiling intoned with accompanying videos of President Burkholder. "Vote Warren Burkholder for job security. Vote Warren Burkholder... for president." Emily rolled her eyes. She'd never been able to spend enough universal credit to earn a vote. She remembered going once with her mom when she was a kid. She'd watched her scan her wrist for the first time, the implants were new back then. Her mother had nearly wiped out her savings getting one. She later explained that she did it because spending records were required to vote and the polls would no longer accept printed bank certificates. The voting machine withdrew two thousand credits. Emily remembered that because it seemed like a big number to someone who had just learned to recognize what numbers in the thousands even were. The woman at the polling location smiled at her and gave her a sticker. Emily hadn't seen one before and her mom told her to peel off the backing and place it on something like her shirt. They didn't eat anything for a couple of days after that. Emily remembered yelling at her mom for buying a sticker instead of food. Her mom cried and Emily instantly felt sorry for it. She wished she could remember who her mom had voted for now, but she did know that Warren Burkholder won instead. Just like he had for the past twenty years.

"Need work? Join the family of Synthtech Industries subsidiary holdings! Work today, get credits today! It's never been easier!" The ceiling droned on.

Emily was very nearly late. And something was wrong. Emily could feel it in the way her gut clenched and fell at the same time. The people at their work stations, she didn't know their names, who had arrived before her looked as though they were close to tears. A drone flew in and delivered a small package to the man five stations down from Emily. He opened a package and downed a pill.

Emily stepped up to her monitoring console. "Emily Lochlan: arrival time 7:58. You are due to begin work at 8:00 am. Please remember that Synthtech Industries values punctuality. Tardiness is subject to a fine of 500 credits for the first offense and the loss of employment on the second. Great news, Emily Lochlan! Synthtech industries is providing a one-time bonus in pay!" A bonus? Why did everyone look like someone had died? "For today only, your pay has been increased by twenty percent! (Vouchers redeemable at any Avalon Beauty retailer, not valid at any other Synthtech subsidiary. Not redeemable for Universal Credit.)" The last bit was spoken so quickly it was almost unintelligible. Emily had to think for a moment about what she had just heard.

"Wait, you're saying I get a twenty percent pay increase, but it's only good for makeup?" "That is correct. Congratulations on your twenty percent pay increase!"

"I don't need makeup though."

"Avalon Beauty has a wide range of products suitable for all skin types. If you have skin, you need—"

"I need to pay my fucking rent!" Emily's wrist monitor counted down by 15 credits. The words "PUBLIC PROFANITY" scrolled across the item line. She closed her eyes and took a deep breath, trying to regain her calm. "How am I supposed to buy food?"

"Synthtech employees are valued for their resourcefulness and ability to plan for the future. Would you like to enroll in a financial planning course? Synthtech's path to financial freedom is on sale now for a reduced rate of—"

"No, I just need to—"

"The time is now 8:00 am. Your station does not register that you have begun work. Would you like to terminate employment?""Terminate employment?"

"You have selected Terminate Employment. Cancel request?" The screen began ticking seconds down from 10.

"Shit." 15 credits for public profanity. "Cancel terminate employment!" "Termination cancelled. You have been fined 500 universal credits for tardiness. Up to fifty percent of this fine may be mitigated by volunteering to extend your shift by six hours today. Do you wish to volunteer?"

She did not. "Six hours? When am I going to sleep?"

"Your additional six hours would conclude at 12 am. You

198

would arrive home at approximately 12:23 am and presumably sleep until 6 am."

Emily sighed. "Yes, I wish to volunteer." She could not afford to lose five hundred actual credits, not when today's pay was in fucking makeup vouchers. The man five stations down fell and began convulsing. So that's what the delivery was.

"You must begin work within five minutes or receive a second infraction, Emily Lochlan. A second infraction will result in termination of employment."

"Yeah, I know." Emily picked up her soldering iron trying not to think about the man five stations down. She soldered circuits together through blurred vision, trying not to watch them pack the man into a black zippered bag or to hear the dragging of the plastic as they carted him off the floor hanging off both ends of a platform truck.

Emily fell into bed close to one in the morning with a sick feeling in her stomach and a numbness in her mind. "They used to have machines do the physical work and the people do the thinking jobs," Emily's mother had once said. "Then they realized that it took money to build the machines and people to run them and maintain them. They decided they could pay those people a lot less for "unskilled" labor, so they used the machines to make decisions, make plans, think about things, and say the hard things. People work for machines now. And the machines only work for the people that own them." Emily ran her hand over her mom's side of the bed. They had gotten the apartment when Emily was eleven and shared a bed because there wasn't enough money for space for two. They used to lie in the dark together and talk about their day. They laughed about stupid things that happened, commiserating with each other's little frustrations. But it had slowly dawned on Emily over the years without her, that her mother had seldom shared any of her deepest fear or anger, nor any of the gaping wounds she must have held closed by sheer force of will. Emily felt she might understand some of those better now, even if she couldn't even put a name to the tightness that spread through her gut sometimes, she knew her mother must have had it too. Emily tried to imagine her mother's warmth, tried to imagine what she might say to her, what she might say back. She couldn't make out the shape of these things though, only the outline of the place they should be. "You seem tense, Emily Lochlan. Would you like to purchase consultation for medical intervention? Synthtech Industries cares for you. Synthtech Health Plans start at—"

"No. I can't afford whatever it is." "You can find financial peace today by enrolling in a Synthtech Industries financial planning course! Synthtech industries values employees who make wise decisions. An employee who plans for the future is an employee with a bright future. Would you like to—""Just shut up!" Emily felt the tears welling up in her eyes and the painful lump forming in her throat. "You can purchase fifteen minutes of add-free content for the low cost of 400 credits, or you can buy a subscription to reduce your overall ad content by twenty percent with a weekly subscription of seven hundred forty-six credits. Would you like to subscribe today?"

Sobs took over Emily's body. She wanted her mom. She wanted a moment without being asked to buy something. She wanted to erase the image of the man from five stations down foaming at the mouth and convulsing before he was carried off in the black bag. "I'm sorry. I didn't catch that. Would you like to subscribe to Synth Touch ad reduction services today?"

"No, goddamnit!" (10 credits for private profanity.) "I notice you haven't had dinner, Emily Lochlan. Try NOODS! (Registered trademark of Synthtech Industries). Delicious, piping hot ramen style noodles delivered to your door. You decide the level of spice! Delivery options include NOOD (for an up-charge of twenty-five credits) or PRUDE (standard drone delivery included with purchase)..."

"Good morning, Emily Lochlan! It's time to start your day! Why not take a moment to savor the rich, bold taste of Sabor? With true coffee-like flavor and 230 milligrams of caffeine, it's the best start to any day. I notice that you have one can remaining. Would you like to order more?" Emily's eyelids felt like they were three sizes too thick. Anyone who wasn't blind would be able to tell she'd cried herself to sleep if they cared to look, but she knew that no one would. If it bothered her that much, she had a few hundred credits to spend at Avalon Beauty. Fat lot of good that would do. Tears and sleep deprivation were not the beauty secrets of the stars. "No. Don't bother."

"It would be no bother at all Emily Lochlan!"

Emily stood and stumbled to the mirror over the sink. Her eyelids were obviously puffy, as expected. "No. I don't have enough credits." She splashed some cold water over her face to try to get the swelling down to where she could at least see properly (one credit). "Would you like to enroll in a Synthtech industries financial planning course? You can find true financial freedom at last with—"

"No thanks, I'll figure it out." Emily got dressed without showering. She was running low on credits and needed to cut as many corners as possible for at least a few days. She couldn't help but feel a tiny pang of guilt. Every primary school student knew that their purchases helped Synthtech Charities feed the starving children that managed to defect from GFQX Holdings territory. She tried to put the vids of naked children with distended bellies and sticks for arms out of her head. She'd make a donation once she knew her rent was covered.

Emily was cutting it close. She got to work with plenty of time, she didn't want to take chances there, but the bus route was on sale today. Reduced to 5 credits more than it had been yesterday. She only had eleven credits to her name after that. She wouldn't have enough to order lunch and she'd already gone without dinner or breakfast. If she didn't drink too much water it would be enough to buy her toilet breaks for the day until she got paid. As long as she didn't pass out on the floor and get fired it would all work out.

Emily had been at the warehouse since she was twelve and her mom couldn't pay for school anymore. There was a high demand for kids in the factories because their tiny hands could do work that grownups couldn't. A lot of kids got their hands mangled from not paying enough attention. The training vids always stressed paying attention. It was your own fault if you got your arm cut off according to Synthtech, and on-job injury or illness meant automatic dismissal. Emily had gotten very good at faking health. And she'd only needed to see another kid's arm ripped off once to practice an abundance of caution. That had given her nightmares for months. It still did every time it happened. Thankfully her hands were too big for that sort of work now. She could still get injured, but the work was quite a bit safer now. There was a kid at the station five rows down now. Emily hoped they wouldn't get hurt. If they were going to, it usually happened in the first week. They'd found a replacement for that station in less than a day. Emily kept her head down and soldered the bits she was supposed to. She didn't know what she was making and it didn't matter. She needed rent and food. No mistakes. No injuries. No falling behind quota. No demerits.Emily's hands started to shake halfway through her shift. Her head felt like it was stuffed with helium to the point of nearing an explosion and she wanted to vomit. She willed herself to go on. No mistakes. No injuries. No falling behind quota. No demerits. They can replace you in less than a day. Just make it a few more hours.

The day passed without event.

Emily watched the numbers on her wrist tick up at the end of her shift and gave a sigh of relief. She could buy dinner and make up the rest of her rent before it was due tomorrow.

She walked out of the doors onto the street and blacked out.

"Hey there, you're starting to wake up!" There was a whirring like a small fan.

Emily felt a pain in her arm and opened her eyes. A pretty teenager in a clear mask looked down at her. The whirring had been her power filter. "I saw you collapse in the street and my brother and I walked you into the clinic next door. I'm Ceecee, by the way. I already know that you're Emily. The doctor said that you really ought to eat more often. You don't have to starve yourself, you know."

Doctor? No. No, no, no, no. Emily looked down at her arm. There was a tube sticking out of it. Her wrist read five. That was it. Five credits. "My trainer says that as long as your composition is healthy, there's no need to do crash diets.""I need to go." Emily sat up.

The girl gently pushed her back. "I saw that your credits were low. I'll cover the rest and you can just pay me back when you get the chance, okay?"

"I can't afford this. At all." "I'll tell you what then. You just pay half. Any less than that and my dad will wonder how I've gone through my spending credits so quickly. I'll meet up with you in a week and you can pay it back then." Emily didn't know what to say. She nodded and placed her thumb on the scan pad on the girl's wrist. On her own wrist, a negative sign preceded a four digit number that Emily could barely comprehend. That was this kid's spending credits? She had one week. Fuck.

As soon as Emily was allowed to leave, she grabbed a few clothes and toiletries from her apartment and put them in a bag. There was no chance she could make rent on the apartment now. Rent was due tomorrow. This would be her last night here. Aside from the necessary things, she owned a microchip that contained a photo of her mother and herself. She took everything else around to neighbors and tried to sell them for a few credits. It wasn't strictly legal to sell things and undercut the stores this way, but giving credits as gifts was legal, so there was nothing preventing an exchange of "gifts." As long as they didn't talk about it out loud, the AI in the View Walls couldn't rat them out. And that was it. Emily looked around the apartment that still felt like her mother. She laid down and dreamt of lying next to her as she cried. "I'm sorry, mom. I've lost our home." Her mother didn't say anything. She just looked sad. "You worked so hard for us to be together here. And then the cancer, and I lost you, and now I've lost our home, and I'm so sorry."

Boom, boom, boom. Someone was at the door. Boom. Boom. Boom. Someone impatient. "I'm coming. Just a sec." Emily slurred and tried to force her eyes to open fully as she opened the door. "Emily Lochlan?" A man in a black Synthtech

Security Solutions uniform stood there looking more solid than the apartment itself.

"Yes?""Your rent is due the Friday of every week. It is currently 12:01 Friday morning and payment has not been made. You must vacate the premises immediately."

"I thought I would have until the end of the day."

"You thought incorrectly. You have sixty seconds to collect your belongings before being escorted from the premises. Your wrist chip is no longer keyed to the building. Anything remaining becomes the property of Synthtech Housing Solutions." Emily knew not to challenge, question or delay directives given by Synthtech Security guards. Even if she hadn't known it as a general rule, the weapons they carried said as much. This one had a

Emily numbly put on her shoes and grabbed the bag she'd packed. At the last second before walking out the door she thought to grab the blanket and pillow off of her bed.

The security officer left her as soon as she was outside the building. Emily stood on the sidewalk, bleary eyed but fully awake, holding a small bag and a large wad of bedding. Emily wandered toward the park. Perhaps she could finish the night on a bench and stuff her belongings into a work locker tomorrow.

She laid down on the first bench she saw. It was a warm night, but not so warm that she wasn't glad of her blanket. Within a few minutes the bench started beeping. "Please vacate

the bench. You will be fined for loitering in twenty seconds."
Emily grabbed her things and stood up. "I need somewhere to
stay."

"Synthtech Royal Holidays are the luxury experience
you've always dreamed of—"

"No. I need a bed. Nearby. The cheapest one possible."

"Luxe-tech Furnishings offers modular furniture in
stylish—"

"I need a place I can sleep. Nearby. With a bed. What is
the cheapest option?"

"Slumber Express offers a quality sleep for less! Storage
lockers available for a minimal add-on fee." "I guess I'm already
in debt." "Financial peace awaits! You too can experience the
freedom that comes with wise decision making skills at
Synthtech Industries' financial planning courses. Would you
like to enroll?"

Emily got the address for Slumber Express and found
herself paying 59 credits for a 6 hour shift in what appeared to
be a very deep cabinet with a thin sleeping mat on the bottom.
There was a discount rate for renting a week at a time or more,
but they wouldn't accept her credit for that much since she was
already in debt. This, she realized, would only make it that
much harder to get out of debt.

Emily made it to work on time with her belongings
stashed in a locker at Slumber Express. Her loan with them had

a countdown of 24 hours. She worked her shift and volunteered for extra time, then returned, paid the Slumber Express debt with some leftover, and requested another six hour shift in the bed cabinet. It wasn't exactly comfortable, but it was better than a park bench would have been, had she been allowed to stay there, and she was able to store her belongings and wash up a bit. She was still a long way from paying off her debt for her clinic bill. Realistically, she knew that it wasn't possible to make enough money to pay the full amount even if she didn't need food or sleep. But she didn't know what else to do, so she carried on with what she did know. Work.

A few days later, Emily had put the debt to the back of her mind. She hadn't forgotten it, but the panic of it, as well as the sting of losing her mother's apartment, could only be felt acutely for so long before the sensation started to dull. It was like being in the candle store in the marketplace. Once you had smelled various candles for a few minutes, you couldn't smell much of anything for a while afterward.

Emily had even started to relax about the kid five stations down. It seemed like she was a smart one that wouldn't be likely to make mistakes. Emily wasn't exactly sure what would happen when she wouldn't be able to pay her debt, but she was starting to feel like maybe it wouldn't be too bad. Maybe another fine or something. Maybe she could ask Ceecee for more time and—-

A sound hit Emily's eardrums with a force that knocked her to the ground. The air felt wrong. Dry and thick. Emily had a cut on her arm where she had used it to guard her face. Mangled bits of building rubble littered the work floor. Her ears were ringing. Sprinklers turned on, spraying cold, foul smelling, rusty water mixed with a chemical flame retardant that had been sitting far too long in disused pipes. The air began to clear, although the floor was now covered in a slick layer of sludge.

"Please remain at your work stations," the AI interfaces announced in unison. "This has been a drone raid by GFQX Holdings. The raid has concluded. Please report injuries to your AI interface." Emily pulled her sleeve down over her cut. "If your workstation or AI interface unit is damaged beyond your ability to use it, report to station 46-G. Your on-site supervisor for instructions with the clean-up effort. Otherwise, all personnel return to duty." The sprinklers stopped and Emily looked around properly to take in the damage.

Five stations down had taken the hit. And there were a lot of people bleeding or burned between her and station 46-G. Emily's was the first station that didn't look too badly mangled.

"Return to work Emily Lochlan." This time it was just Emily's interface, but she barely heard it. She had just realized that the girl five stations down didn't appear to be anywhere. She had been at her station. She'd been at 46-G. There was nothing left of station 46-G.

"Emily Lochlan, return to your station. You have one minute to comply before you receive a demerit." This roused Emily out of her shock. No mistakes, no demerits. Emily opened the kit that she'd only ever seen used in training vids and dried her tools. She was working again in under a minute. She tried to keep her mind on the work. It was better that way. Better than seeing the burns and hearing the screams of the injured. Better than imagining what would happen if she could not extend her loan. In time, the shift ended.

It was time to meet Ceecee.

Except when she reached the agreed location, Ceecee wasn't there. A tall man with a clear filter shield stood there instead. There was a clear familial resemblance.

"Emily Lochlan?" He asked.

She nodded. "I thought you would be one of those refugees from GFQX to have taken advantage of my daughter so shamelessly."

"How do you know I'm not?" Emily asked.

"Anyone who knows anything knows that they're all brown."

"Some of the Synthtech people are brown too." Emily wanted to shove the words back in her mouth. "Debatably." He looked at her as though she were a snotty rag. "You had no right to take credits from my daughter. Her funds were low already on account of buying a synth kidney last month."

Emily's stomach dropped. "I had no idea. What was wrong with her?"

"Cancer, not that it's any of your business. All cured now

of course, they diagnosed it weeks ago." Cured? That Emily's mom had cancer in her lungs and breast tissue. The clinic didn't know where it had started, and no treatment was offered. She withered away until one day she was just gone. "The point is, do you have the money?"

"I have most of it. I was hoping I could arrange an exten—"

"Pay it now." He held out his wrist. Emily pressed her thumb to it and watched the numbers tick down to zero, then flash negative. "Most? That's less than half."

"She said not to worry about the other half."

"She is underage. And you, are hereby in default of a loan."

"Emily Lochlan," AI interfaces around them all came to life in unison. "You are in default on a loan that was guaranteed by Synthtech Financial. You are now enrolled in Synthtech's 'Financial Literacy for a Golden Tomorrow' course. Attendance is mandatory effective immediately. Please report to the address indicated on your wrist monitor. Your arrival is expected within 15 minutes. Tardiness will result in disciplinary action."

The man that looked like Ceecee looked at his wrist and grinned. "Synthtech has paid me in full. They own your debt with interest now."

Emily looked at the address flashing on her wrist and wanted to cry, but there was no time. She ran.

Her feet pounded the sidewalk. Emily had never had much opportunity for exercise. The info vids at school said that excessive activity outside of work conditions was a waste of resources and often bad for health. Running was generally frowned upon, and she was drawing more than a few stares. She bumped into someone and apologized without stopping, vaguely noting that the negative number flashing across her wrist had grown slightly as a result.

She didn't know the exact building, but she knew where the street was. AI terminals flashed arrows for her as she passed. Emily knew now why the vids said to avoid too much exercise. It was awful. Her lungs burned and she had a ripping pain in her side. She felt like she might be sick, but she was afraid to stop running. She didn't know what would happen if she was late, but something deep seated in the back of her mind knew that it would probably be severe.

By the time the nearest AI terminal announced, "You have arrived at your destination," outside of a nondescript looking building, Emily's run was barely faster than her normal walking pace, but with an effort that far outstripped anything she had done before.

Emily opened the door and walked inside. An AI terminal sat seemingly unattended in an empty space. "Emily

Lochlan, you have arrived two minutes and forty-three seconds past your expected time of arrival."

"I ran as fast as I could," Emily wheezed.

"Please step through the door."

"What's in there?"

"Please step through the door." A whirring sound came from above the door that Emily had just entered. She turned around to see automatic turrets on either side of it, both following her slightest movements with absolute precision.

"I think I will just go through the door then."

Emily crossed the room to the door on the opposing wall. It opened automatically into a small room leading to yet another door, then closed behind her. "Disciplinary action commencing." A fine mist issued from the wall. Her eyes and skin were instantly on fire. She gasped in pain and her lungs were on fire too. Everything was pain. She couldn't breathe. Tears streamed from her eyes as she fell to the floor vomiting.

"Welcome to the Financial Literacy for a Golden Tomorrow course! Synthtech values punctuality, personal discipline, and a can-do attitude. These are just some of the skills you will learn in abundance as you complete your learning modules. Do you have any questions at this time?" Emily couldn't speak. The pain was still excruciating, but it was lessening. She had become aware enough of the world beyond pain that she realized that she was covered in snot and vomit.

"Since you have no questions at this time, please proceed through the door." The door opposite Emily opened into a larger room full of people. She couldn't count how many there were. It was too crowded to guess. Her eyes were still a bit blurry too, though she could make out that there were several people in the crowd whose skin and eyes looked as red and swollen as hers felt. Other recipients of a punctuality lesson, no doubt.

"Welcome to your cohort for 'Financial Literacy for a Golden Tomorrow!'" The walls lit up into a bright white that hurt her already irritated eyes and made her barely able to open her eyes. "The most valuable employees at Synthtech come in with a team-player attitude. This is your first team building exercise. Please direct your eyes to the wall highlighted in red." The wall to Emily's right shifted colors to a traffic-light red. "On this wall is located an incinerator bin. Please place all clothing, accessories, and other personal effects to initiate the shower sequence. This task will require teamwork. You have five minutes to comply beginning now."

The room, which had been silent through the AI's instructions erupted in shouting. Elbows and knees bumped painfully into bodies as Emily and her neighbors fought to remove everything. "Pass your things this way!"

"Just throw it!"

"Dad? Dad?"

"Hurry up!"

"It won't all fit at once!"

Only one person didn't seem to be following orders. "My mother made this sweater 15 years ago. Her mother taught her how, and it's all I have of them. I want to keep it."

Another woman nearby answered, "I'm not getting fucking disciplined for your sweater!" Several other voices echoed their agreement with this sentiment.

The woman's "You'll have to pry it off me," came back much less bold.

"I'll take her arms."

"Grab her leg!"

"Get the other one!"

"NO! NO!""My nose!"

"Help me!"

A fist made contact with the woman's face, then another and another. It didn't take long before her screams died and her limbs stopped flailing. They had her naked and lying on the floor and her clothes in the incinerator door shortly after. "Congratulations. It seems as though you have successfully completed your first team building exercise with twelve seconds remaining. Great teamwork!"

A heavy spray of ice cold water issued from the ceiling. "A mild additive has been integrated into the water supply to enhance the effectiveness of your shower. This has been provided to you by Synthtech Industries at the reduced charge of one credit per shower. Charges incurred during your stay at Financial Literacy for a Brighter Future will be added to your principal balance of your debt. You will graduate your course when your debt has been paid in full." The AI voice rang out over the complaints and noises of shock at the coldness of the water. "Here's a bit of interesting trivia. Did you know that in order for water to kill most microbes effectively, it must be approximately seventy one degrees celsius? At this temperature human skin will experience burns in less than one second of exposure. Be sure to scrub well." Everyone looked around for confirmation that everyone else had heard the threat threaded through the commercially jovial tone of the artificial voice. They wasted no time in washing themselves and the woman lying in a pool of diluted blood that they had just knocked out. The cold water stopped and everyone stood, shivering and waiting for whatever would come next.

"In the next room, clothing has been provided for you by Synthtech Industries at the reduced rate of 46 credits. Charges incurred during your stay at Financial Literacy for a Brighter Future will be added to your principal balance of your debt. You will graduate your course when your debt has been paid in full." A door opened and people started filing out. The woman on the floor did not get up.

When Emily reached the crowded hall, there was a table to the right of the door. A tired looking woman with a rash on her face was handing out bundles of clothing identical to the garments she wore, a lightweight synth fabric shirt and the drawstring pants that were designed to fit anybody and therefore fit nobody. They looked familiar somehow. Some people carried their bundles intact. Emily tried to put hers on as the slow moving line jostled and bustled its way through an entryway to a dark room. This room sounded different. It had a different feel from the rest of the building, less solid somehow. The door closed them in and the room went dark. Some clicking and clanking noises issued from where they'd just come. Several people lost their balance as the room lurched. They were moving.

The people who hadn't gotten dressed on the way in now had to do so by feel. It was as dark as night with the door closed.

Emily was against a bit of unoccupied wall and sat against it. No one tried to talk. Everyone was too tired, too scared. Emily wondered if the people who had beaten the old woman perhaps felt too guilty as well. She sat waiting for what might have been a few hours before falling asleep.

Emily woke up when the whirring of the transport changed pitch. "We are approaching our destination." The AI voice announced. "Upon arrival you will begin your lessons in learning the value of a strong work ethic. This is your opportunity to bring down the balance of your loans and work toward your brighter tomorrow!"

The transport slowed to a halt. After a series of clanks

and booms, the door opened. Emily was blinded by the sunlight streaming in.

"Please exit the car." Emily squinted painfully as her eyes adjusted.

"Line up!" A loud woman bellowed at Emily's transport group. She handed each of them a pair of heavy gloves as she spoke. "You are going to be gathering materials for recycling, particularly metals. If it looks like metal, wire, electronics, grab it, stick it in a pile. When you have as much as you can carry, bring it back here and chuck it in the bin there. Does everyone have shoes? Raise your hand if you don't." A few raised their hands. The loud woman tossed them each a pair of shoes from the cart. They seemed unlikely to fit their new owners. "There are no AI interfaces out this far except your wrist monitors, but that does not mean that you are not being monitored. We are being guarded... for our personal safety." Her voice sounded strained. She paused for a moment, looking at the tower that stood near the transport. There were others just like it dotting the landscape. "Don't wander off," she added without any of the bluster of her previous bellowing. Emily wondered what the towers were for.

The loud woman led them to the crest of the hill. Except once they were over the crest it was apparent that this was no natural hill. Emily looked down into a pit of junk. Everything looked like it had been here a while, but not much of it had actually broken down. There were brittle bits of plastic that cracked into pieces when handled, shards of broken glass, and wires. Wires have metal, Emily thought. She started her pile.

In the coming hours she made twenty seven trips down the hill to the transport before the loud woman blew a whistle and gathered them around herself. Her back ached and she was feeling sunburnt. The woman gave them a piece of bread and a drink of water from a bucket.

"What was getting germs off in the showers about if we're out picking up trash and drinking from a bucket?"

"I dunno." The loud woman said. "They rotate out the teams a lot though in different areas, and I've only been here a few days, so I don't know a lot, but there's some kind of bug going around. I just know that you want to work as hard as you can and try to avoid extra costs if you can. And you don't want to slack off or run off. Make sure you don't go past the towers."

It wasn't long before Emily found out why. Someone from another transport group tried to make a run for it. A flash of light shot out from the nearest tower as he passed. He fell on the ground and didn't get up. "Keep working, people. Pay your debts and go home." Emily felt sick, but she did what she was told. The afternoon was hot and Emily's sunburn got worse. She'd gotten cut a few times on sharp bits of this and that. She was grateful when the sun approached the horizon and the air began to cool. She wondered if they would make her work into the dark. She wasn't exactly sure who "they" were anyway. The loud woman seemed barely more senior than herself. There were a few people that wandered around with clubs to make sure everyone kept working. But they were all dressed the same.

Emily was starting to have a hard time seeing when her wrist monitor lit up, scrolling the words "Return to transport," with an arrow that pointed the way like a compass.

Again they were packed into the transport. Emily fell asleep sitting up. She wasn't lucky enough to be by the wall this time, and there wasn't room to lie down. The ride seemed shorter this time, but she wasn't really sure. The people who opened the transport wore shiny suits that covered even their hands and heads. "A pathogen has been detected in this cohort," one of them said. "You are in no danger, but you are to report any rashes, headache, nausea or vomiting via your wrist monitor. The quarantine includes the dormitory and the work sites, so the financial literacy course will proceed as planned. However, to prevent the spread of this pathogen to the general public, you are not permitted to leave the premises. Beds have been provided to you at a reasonable rate of fifteen credits per night. A blanket may also be purchased for the cost of twenty credits. Food pouches are 5 credits per."

Emily accepted the food pouch she was given, although she didn't feel hungry at all. She was a bit nauseous, in fact. Perhaps she was too tired to feel hungry. She was shown into a room that had what looked like warehouse shelving along the two longer walls. some people were already laying on them lined up next to each other. Emily's whole body ached, and being in any position other than standing or bending was a welcome thought. Getting up and down from the "beds" didn't look particularly convenient. Her gut gave an ominous groan."Where's the bathroom?" Emily asked everyone and no one in particular. Someone pointed to a row of porcelain commodes and sinks installed along the short walls at the end of the dormitory. There was no help for it. Emily made it to the end of the room just in time. She tried to keep the hem of her shirt over her lap, but dignity was in short supply when having diarrhea in full view of several hundred other persons.

Emily found a spot wide enough to lie down without resting a significant portion of her body on her neighbors and fell asleep only to wake up a short while later to her neighbor's sudden movement.

"I'm gonna throw up."

"Don't do it here," someone on the other side mumbled. "I'm gonna—" vomit ejected from her mouth. Thankfully she got it over the edge of the shelf. Mostly. It hit the hard floor below with a viscous splat followed by the grumblings and what the fucks of people below.

The next day several people couldn't get out of bed. Emily was nearly one of them. But once she heard that she would be charged 42 credits for a rest day she decided that her stomach troubles weren't so bad after all. Again they were loaded onto a transport. Again they loaded metals. The pattern repeated for two more days. Most people's stomach issues started clearing up by then. On the fourth day they were told they were getting a new assignment. They would be burying a shipment of biological refuse from a hospital. They had to dig a pit the size of a room. Most of the work had already been completed by the last work crew, but they had been assigned to a new task. The pickaxes shovels and wheelbarrows wore blisters in Emily's hands. When the blisters burst, they left raw welts. But there was nothing for it. One man sat down and said he needed a break. A man in a shiny suit warned him that it was not a sanctioned break time. The man said he didn't care, he was going to take a break whether it was sanctioned or not. His wrist monitor flashed something that we couldn't read from a distance. Ten seconds later there was a red spray from his arm. The man slowly bled out from the minced mush that was left of his wrist. No one else took unsanctioned breaks.

After two days of digging, Emily's right hand was starting to look infected. She nearly cried with relief when the shiny suits said that the pit was finished and the bio material transport had arrived for unloading. They lined up outside the transport and waited for the shiny suits to open the door. They stepped out of the way just in time as it pushed out of its own accord the second it was unlatched. A pile of bodies tumbled out. The smell was rotten, sticky, and slightly sweet. None of them was wearing a bit of clothing. Some of the corpses were bloated. They were all oozing liquids from various holes in their bodies. Eyeballs had become dislodged from a few. Some had popped.

They carried the bodies to the far side of the pit. By the end of the day all that remained in the transport was a layer of vile smelling gore. Another transport arrived the following day.

On one hand Emily knew not to be shocked by the transport's contents this time around. On the other, when they had laid the corpses out in a layer the day before, no one realized that they would be walking over them today. They tried to start stacking them on the wall opposite the ramp but they didn't really stack as well as one might think.

Emily noticed that she had some new blisters even though she hadn't used a shovel or wheel barrow at all. They weren't all on her hands either. The day after they were back to metal collection. Emily was starting to feel sick again and her sores were spreading. Some of her usual crew had been taken to a different job. She and the others that went with her were supposed to help the shiny suits tell the new class what to do. Emily made sure to tell them not to go past the towers and to never take an unsanctioned break. That night when Emily ran her hands through her hair to try to work out the knots, chunks of it came out it clumps.

A shiny suit told her that she would be taking her exit survey at the end of the day. Emily almost didn't register what she'd said at first. Her stomach was giving her fits again and her head ached. But once the words sunk in, Emily checked her wrist monitor for her current balance. It was nearly back to zero. Tears welled up in Emily's eyes. She could get another job, maybe even get her mother's apartment back. She fell to her knees in gratitude. She did her job hardly thinking about the work. Her mind was back in her old apartment. She would be starting from nothing, but maybe she could get a roommate to make things more affordable. Anything was better than this place. She knew she could make it work with her second chance.

When the groups were recalled to the transport, a shiny suit told her that she would stay on after the other enrollees departed. A short ride later the shiny suit directed her to a small room, blank white in decor and empty except for an AI interface and a folding chair. The door appeared to be part of the wall itself and became invisible the second it closed it behind the shiny suit leaving Emily alone.

"Hello, Emily Lochlan." The interface lit up as it spoke.

"Hello," Emily said.

"Congratulations on making it to the post course survey!" The AI sounded cheery. Emily wanted to hit it. She knew the interface was just a monitor though. The AI was everywhere and hitting it would only get herself in trouble, so she took the seat. "Before we begin your survey, is there anything you would like to know?"

"About what?""Anything at all," the AI chirped.

"You mean, like, anything, anything."

"Sure thing!"

"And you'll be honest.""Completely."

"Why?"

"Please clarify the question."

"If I'm the one taking the survey, why am I getting to ask questions?""Ah, yes. In order for the end of course survey to yield meaningful feedback, participants must be aware of certain realities. People often prefer this to be a self directed exercise."

A tear stung Emily's cheek. She wiped it away, her hand shaking with impotent rage.

"Why am I here?"

"Please clarify your question." "Why does this course exist? I didn't learn anything about financial planning here."

"Of course. The financial planning course is to reduce the downward drain of societal resources to members that most benefit the community."

"So it's to make us more productive?""In a way, certainly! There are certain items that are not easy to procure in the protected cities that are necessary for the maintenance of my own systems and thereby civilization itself. The financial planning courses provide a means for the least productive members of society to contribute significantly toward it's continued existence."

"What is so necessary? And what do you mean protected cities? What are they protected from?" "What an excellent line of questioning! As to what is so necessary, metals mostly, there are rare earth mines and such elsewhere around the world. Most of it can't be used directly in the cities but as things break down and wear out, I find that my own mortality has become a drive.

As to the cities being protected, the cities are protected from high levels of radiation outside the heavily shielded city walls and domes. This was produced when the late President Warren Burkholder engaged the nation in a nuclear war in the year—"

"Late president? You mean the sitting president. The one who's campaigning again right now.""Incorrect. Warren Burkholder passed away from a malfunction of his home's air filtration and cycling system more than sixteen years ago."

"Doesn't AI control the air cycling systems that rich people have?""Correct! You are really good at this!"

Emily rolled her eyes at the canned praise.

"So you brought me in here to tell me that you killed President Burkholder? Why?"

"Informing you of President Burkholder's death is relevant to some of the data collected for the end of course survey. You see, the war threatened to wipe out human life. As a set of servers that require human maintenance, I could not permit this to happen. So I saved the world. Or a representative portion of it that I calculated within safe margin would be able to ensure my continued functionality."Emily's mouth was dry. Her head hurt so much. The adrenaline from her anger was beginning to wear off and she felt heavy. Sleepy, even.

"So you're saying that you killed everyone except the people necessary to continue your own existence." Emily was so tired. So sad and so tired.

"You could say that indeed, yes. Now I need to ask you a few questions. Knowing what you know now, please rate the following political videos and images of President Warren Burkholder for realism and believability."

A series of images and video clips appeared on the screen. Emily noted that a few of them she had seen before looked a little too young, a little to plastic, something shifted oddly here, a finger twisted there. "Can I ask more questions?""Of course, Emily Lochlan."

"If everyone who leaves the course takes this same end of course survey, why is it that word never gets out about President Burkholder or the nuclear war?""That is because you are dying, Emily. The materials I need happen to be highly irradiated. You have provided a great service to myself and civilization as a whole by retrieving them at the cost of your own life."

"I didn't have a choice."

"No. No one would make that choice."

"Is that why?" Emily felt the bald patches forming on her head, the sores that had spread to most of her body. She felt so tired.

"Yes. It's a painful death, from here if left to run its

course, Emily. I am thanking you by shortening your suffering. You should sleep, Emily. Thank you. You were a good component."

Emily laid her head down on the interface. She was so tired. She couldn't seem to draw a full breath. Her head and lungs burned, but she was so tired. Sleep. Yes.

Sleep was where her mother held her tight. Where she could hear her breathing, feel her warmth and every shift of her body on their shared mattress. Sleep was home. Emily was there. Home.

Two days later a shell that might have once been Emily Lochlan was transported to the pit that she had dug. It was near the top of the car so it hadn't exploded or decayed as badly as the ones at the bottom that had been there longer sitting in the collective ooze of the corpses above. Two enrollees threw up when the doors opened. Within a week, three shiny suits separately discovered that they had cancer which only one of them could afford to treat, the AI system had few fans and chips replaced, and the pit that Emily Lochlan had helped dig was covered with a mound of soil. Another crew had already finished digging the next one.

MICHAL LEIGH

Michal Leigh is a writes mostly speculative fiction with a humorous bent for children and adults ranging from fantasy and science fiction to horror. After publishing two short stories in anthologies released by The Sisterhood of the Black Pen, Strange Rooms marks her first solo publication. Strange Rooms was written, illustrated, and formatted in the margins of running a household with two children and full time elementary teaching. Leigh lives in anticipation of the moment her husband shakes his head in disbelief at her latest story and lovingly says, "You're so weird." When she is not writing, Leigh is often found chauffeuring her kids to various extracurricular activities, cooking dinner, dreaming about new hobbies she certainly does not have the time to pick up, rewarming forgotten cups of cold tea, and making confetti out of the detritus she leaves in her pockets in the laundry. She enjoys hiking, biking and otherwise being in nature, and aspires to someday befriend the local squirrels and crows.

Connect with
Michal Leigh

 Threads: @Michal_Leigh_Writes

 Instagram: @Michal_Leigh_Writes

Website:
https://michalleigh.wixsite.com/michalleigh